TAMING THE CHINESE DRAGON

YOUNG LOVE IN CHANGING TIBET

AN HISTORICAL NOVEL

BY JULIAN NAVA

WPR BOOKS
CARLSBAD, CA

THE BOOK CREATION TEAM

Editing Assistance: Todd Mattox
                        Marjorie Rodgers
Cover Photo: Shutterstock
Publisher: Kirk Whisler

For more about books presented by WPR Publishing, please go to www.WPRbooks.com.

WPR BOOKS
3445 Catalina Dr., Carlsbad, CA 92010-2856
www.WPRbooks.com 760-434-1223 kirk@whisler.com

Table of Contents

CHARACTERS IN NOVEL WHOSE LIFE EMBODIES CHANGING TIBET

Pasang ~ A patriotic boy flees to Nepal where he lives with a woman for years while pinning away for his love back in Tibet.

Indus ~ Tibetan girl sold by family, longs for Pasang, doing anything to raise their son, while longing for his return

Chang ~ Tibetan nobleman buys Indus and thrives doing business with new occupying regime.

Ola ~ Chang's older mistress mentors young Indus in love so Indus can please her master Chang

Taos ~ Pasang's friend and young monk at old monastery explains Buddhist life as retreat from the sordid world

Torfu ~ terrible gang-leader befriends Pasang

Tara ~ Nepalese woman shelters Pasang as his lover and mentor for years, dreading his eventual departure

Lieutenant Li ~ Chinese occupying officer Indus takes in and loves Indus, as she privately pines away for Pasang

Pasang Junior ~ raised by Lieutenant Li who sponsors his education like a son

Chu ~ talkative girl student nurse captures Pasang's love

Old Professor ~ explains the global context of China's control in changing Tibet amid major power struggles

Introduction

I want the reader to understand the changes taking place in the Himalayas since the People's Republic of China took control of Tibet in 1950. While visiting China, north of Korea in Jilin Province, and Tibet far south as well, I listened to ordinary people and heard many views about current global affairs. As a world traveler and university Professor of History, I concluded that thoughtful readers would enjoy knowing more about Tibet than the little that regular media tells about.

I decided that a historical novel was the best way to tell about what is happening in Tibet in an entertaining way that a novel permits. The love story is buried within actual events and facts. Indeed, some episodes of the novel contain unknown information I learned from CIA sources while serving as a U.S. ambassador.

The world has followed the drama of the Dalai Lama and his efforts to preserve Tibet's ancient autonomy. As winner of the Nobel Peace Price, the Dalai Lama enjoys the respect and sympathy of people around the globe. The events in Tibet are complicated and provoke valid conflicting evaluations of China's role, which the novel portrays. The author hopes that his story helps promote greater understanding and good will, while telling a moving and unusual love story that embodies the events that have taken place in Tibet.

I hope you enjoy the novel,

Julian Nava

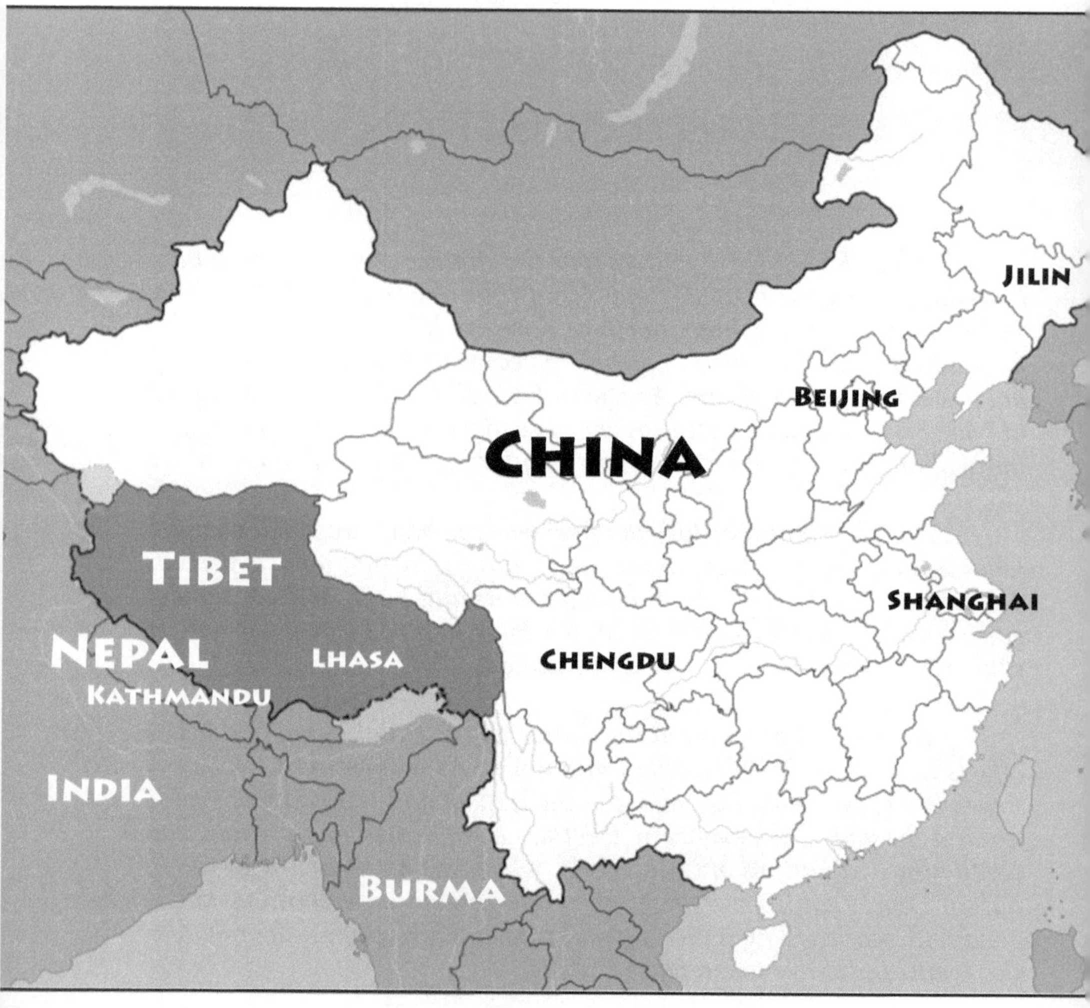

JILIN
BEIJING
CHINA
SHANGHAI
TIBET
NEPAL
LHASA
KATHMANDU
CHENGDU
INDIA
BURMA

CHAPTER ONE

Forbidden Love

A Tibetan boy hurries up the trail towards Nepal in late fall leaving his home in Lhasa behind, perhaps forever. He must avoid a looming storm that could trap him and the gang of smugglers he has joined. The Dokar Pass is one of many known for trader activity, as well as bandits. Young Pasang is happy to be with the men he has paid to guide him over the Himalayas. All at once snow starts to fall and he can barely see ahead.

Pasang is tired and stumbles down a slope. The smugglers hardly give him a glance as they trudge on, intent on reaching shelter before dark. Some of the men exchange words about Pasang as the snowfall thickens. The leader cuts them off. They have what they wanted, Pasang had already paid for help escaping from Tibet, and so the men keep going on. Pasang is left behind.

That he is alone in a snowstorm takes hold of him. It's getting dark and the worsening snowfall further blurs his path ahead, so he prepares a small hut of ice and snow in which he will sleep in hopes of waking up at dawn. This technique for survival was familiar to his people. He curls up tight and tries to relax in order to use less energy to ward off the cold. Pasang starts to meditate by softly chanting a Buddhist prayer over and over. He remembers the power of meditation he learned from a monk friend not long ago. Although not sure of its value at the time, now he thought he might as well try it, deciding to have faith that through meditation he could gain control over his body, and thus withstand the cold. Talking to himself, he is glad that at least he has shelter from the wind outside. Pasang accepts that he will either wake up in the morning or not. His fate is in the hands of the mountain gods, in any case. He had doubts about the gods, as well as the value of meditation, but again, why not believe in the gods now?

Snow gradually covers his little hut and quietly protects him. No one could find him, not even Chinese patrols. He is completely on his own. Pasang murmurs the prayer over and over, but before long he is mixing up the words. He starts the prayer over to no avail. He is hallucinating and starts to relive an important episode of his life.

Pasang is walking in the countryside on a summer day. Suddenly he sees a lovely girl. She is running away from an older man. Pasang recognizes Chang, a wealthy landowner. The old man is muttering to himself about this disrespectful young girl he wants to purchase. However, Chang takes the chase in stride as a sort of game. The chase actually inflames his desire for the girl even more. But by now he feels that enough is enough. The man is growing impatient.

Pasang responds to the girl's urgent pleas for help as the old man comes closer. He takes hold of the girl and pushes her out of view up on top of some boulders. He cannot help but see her lovely bottom as he pushes her up. It's a fleeting glance that will last his lifetime. He tells the man that she went another way. On the rocks, Indus just holds her breath. She asks to come down after a while. He lets her slide down face away and cups her small breasts on purpose, holding on to her longer than necessary. She turns around and looks at him curiously, but is not concerned about his bold touch. She is worried about the old man walking away in the distance, and makes some surprisingly nasty remarks about him.

Pasang persuades her to stop whimpering. He asks about her flight and she explains that her parents intend to sell her to Chang. Like many poor Tibetan families, extra boys or girls were sold into servitude. Pasang tells her "As your owner, he can do whatever he likes with you." "Yes, I know," she replies. " But I don't see what he wants me for, I am barely a woman." Pasang regards her intently. As a member of a noble family, Chang is a powerful man in the Lhasa valley. Chang could buy any of a number of girls. He already has two women living with him for many years; no one knew if they were his wives or just servants. It would be quite ordinary if he wanted to add a young girl to his household as a plaything.

For Pasang it is love at first sight. His look hides growing affection as she chatters away. When she takes a breath, he cuts in, "I know that we can only be friends, but perhaps can we meet again sometime to talk?" His question makes her look intently at him for the first time. He is tall, dark, and his face is already slightly wrinkled, as is common in the harsh climate of Tibet. He is handsome. She likes his voice and commanding manner. He likes her liveliness and that she talks back to him as an equal. The pair part and go their own ways before the old man returns.

The next day they meet near a cold stream where many girls wash clothes. The tall rocks where yesterday she had taken shelter were nearby. Some women trudge by slowly on a trail with bundles of firewood on their backs. Their men walk ahead, ignoring the women except to scold them to hurry. Pasang and Indus become acquainted sitting down beside the cold stream, with the enormous Himalayan peaks above. They converse about their families and livelihoods. Both live on farms belonging to nobles, not far apart. Although each family has a small plot to farm, their noble can call upon them for labor or services whenever he wants. He also collects a part of their annual crops. They live in mud huts with dirt floors upon which they sleep curled up tight on wool blankets. Tibetan families are small. Pasang is an only child, while Indus has two brothers. The landlords do not want more people than the land can support. The young couple do not question the way things are.

Pasang is clearly in love, but he plays the traditional male role of dominating women and treating them as subservient. Young Indus, however, has not yet learned her role as an obedient girl and so she talks freely as an equal. Her confident manner and easy laugh reveal a strong personality that captivates Pasang. Indus talks back to him when she disagrees and reveals an inquisitive nature. He loves to hear her talk.

Time passes, and Indus went to live in the house of Chang. Not long after the move, the pair met again in the original spot near the stream with tall grass alongside. Chang was always away somewhere on business. As they lay out of view in the grass she tells Pasang how her father scolded her for her reservations about the buyer's amorous intentions. Chang had taken notice of her in the village and asked her father to sell her to him. Her father and mother made it clear to Indus that their livelihood depended on their owner's good will. Moreover, Indus told Pasang, her mother told her this was the way of life for women.

In response to Pasang's blunt question, Indus pointed out devilishly that her owner had not gotten what he wanted, at least not yet. When the owner had cornered her in a room, pushed her onto a bed and got down to have her, he could not perform sexually, Indus told Pasang with pleasure. Chang could not maintain an erection stiff enough to enter a tight Indus. She had the good sense not to humiliate Chang. The old man stormed off and has left her alone. Pasang smiled because by now he could, knowing Chang's attempt had failed. He was greatly relieved because Indus told him all this in complete frankness. Chang wanted Indus not only as a plaything, he also hoped that she could give him a son, which he wanted more than anything. The older women living with him could not conceive. That would be her function in his household: a plaything and a mother of his son.

The secret meetings by the stream had become regular. The women washing clothes nearby understood what was going on in the tall grass. There were no longer any secrets between the young pair. The noisy stream covered their talk. Some of the women just shook their heads in sadness. They knew this young couple had a sad future ahead.

The women knew that out of pride Chang would not get rid of Indus even if he found out about Pasang. His sharecroppers knew he had bought her and could guess why. If Chang learned about Pasang and dismissed Indus, rumors about why he dismissed her would soon spread. Chang knew about young Pasang in the village but did not imagine the secret romance. Pasang was too young to realize the terrible risk he was taking with Indus. There was no telling what Chang would do to protect his reputation. Actually, he could do what he liked. As a member of the nobility he could do as he liked with his serfs. They were his property.

The washing women knew the young boy was of little importance. The pretty girl was property to be used for the pleasure of her owner in due time. Meanwhile, Chang had two women who knew how to please him. Pleasure late in life and mostly making money took all his time. While the washer-women fantasized about the young pair, the two enjoyed each other in the shelter of the tall grass. Tibetans usually did their body functions whenever they liked with no public shame. When Indus rode atop Pasang she was visible above the grass. The women just smiled, recalling their youth.

One day after Indus and Pasang had a rendezvous he was walking home full of pleasant memories. Near the village a young monk confronted him. Pasang had nothing to give the monk as an offering. He knew that offerings to monks earned credits in the next life. Tibetans gave of whatever they had whenever they encountered a monk. But Pasang had nothing to share. Coming closer, he recognized the monk as a childhood friend. After greetings, Tao explained that he was a novice at a nearby monastery. They exchanged stories to catch up with each other, after which Tao invited Pasang to visit the monastery. "You don't expect me to join you in the monastery, do you?" Tao replied, "Why not? Who wants anything to do with the world as it is?"

The Tibetan world was changing rapidly as the two friends spoke. The Dalai Lama had learned from the highly regarded Nechung Oracle that it was unsafe for him to stay in his summer palace. Chinese troops were approaching Lhasa from the eastern provinces. The few Tibetan troops did not know what to do. The Chinese protested friendship, and the Tibetan government, although of divided counsel, was willing to reach an agreement with the People's Liberation Army as long as Tibetan freedom was assured. The young Dalai Lama did not know or understand such novel international machinations. The young monk told Pasang about some of these events and why he was content with life as a monk, apart from everyday, ordinary life. Pasang and the public in Tibet knew nothing about the international movements at play.

Very few Tibetans knew about the existence of the United States of America, or therefore about its involvement in Tibetan-Chinese affairs. The CIA was heavily involved in forging a disruptive campaign against China. A few agents working out of Nepal and India were in contact with selected Tibetans, supplying them with arms and money. American activities were so secret that nearby Nepal and India, under Prime Minister Nehru, knew nothing about the American activities.

The United States, along with a coalition in the UN, was engaged in a war in Korea. North Korea, with Chinese support, had launched an invasion of South Korea to make it communist. Much of Asia was in turmoil. On the island of Taiwan, remnants of the Chinese Republic were warding off threats from China, which claimed the island. China denounced American support for Taiwan and American threats to protect its independence. India, for its part, resented increasing American involvement in Asian affairs. It openly denounced American intentions to take the place of England as a superpower in Asia. Actually, India cared little about Taiwan, it was concerned about issues close to home. Border issues with Pakistan and China over Tibet were what made India sensitive about American involvement in that part of the world.

Poor Tibet was a pawn in global affairs. In the midst of all of these conflicting interests, the Dalai Lama fled for safety to India. The Soviet Union, England, the United States, and India all had conflicting interests in Tibet, and the Cold War increased the dangerous tensions. In the midst of all this, Tibet did not have the status of an independent nation. Appeals to the United Nations by Tibetan representatives were taken note of and set aside for discussion later. None of the Security Council members wanted discussions that could lead to decisions about Tibet, not even the United States. Indecision suited all the major powers.

Tibetan monasteries had a surprising chain of information. Tao continued with his account to Pasang. "We don't know where the Dalai Lama will take refuge. He is very young and has two senior advisors teaching him in preparation for his coronation. He must pass some very comprehensive tests before he can be crowned, you know. We do know that he fled at night dressed as a commoner. Several thousand followers traveled with him over the mountains. The flight was very impressive."

Angered over the secret flight of the Dalai Lama, the Chinese forces began a program of revenge. Tao said, "We hear rumors the Chinese will use us to tear down our own monastery, as they have started to do with others, all the more incensed at the flight of the Dalai Lama because so many Tibetans accomplished it in secret." Tao did not go into details about how the Dalai Lama flight came about. He knew it was prudent to keep this to himself.

The true story about the escape revealed that in March the Chinese had invited a select group of Tibetans to attend the performance of dancers from Beijing as part of a cross cultural experience, sharing classical Chinese folklore not familiar to Tibetans. The performance was to take place in the military garrison close to Lhasa. The Dalai Lama's acceptance to attend alarmed numerous lamas and rumors spread that an oracle counseled against his attendance. Men on horseback and bicycles spread the alarm that the Chinese intended to kidnap the Dalai Lama. Perhaps they would take him to China under some diplomatic excuse and deprive Tibetans of their leader. Supporters insisted he should remain in the Summer Palace. Tensions were increasing among those who heard about the invitation made by the Chinese officials. Two secular Tibetan officials were killed due to rumors that they favored acceptance of the invitation. Tibetan upper class individuals were now commonly accused of being Chinese collaborators. For his part, the young Dalai Lama was not afraid. He was rather very curious about Chinese dancing and music. His counselors changed his mind and he left Tibet secretly at night with many supporters that grew in numbers as they proceeded. It was the safer thing to do. The world heard about the flight from an Indian radio station, which announced the presence of the Tibetan leader in India.

"Some Chinese will let us practice our religion as long as we accept their claim to Tibet as part of China," Tao pointed out. "The Chinese are of divided opinion over what to do with us. By the western calendar, 1959 was an "Obstructive year." Everyone should take caution about everything; most of all, someone like the Dalai Lama," Tao said. The Chinese government was greatly offended by the flight of the Dalai Lama, and ascribed many evil intentions to the event. Tibetan elite groups knew nothing about plans for the flight since there were no plans. It was a spontaneous event. Amidst the growing confusion, crowds paraded in support of their spiritual leader and attacked Chinese civilians and soldiers. Under orders to avoid an uprising, Chinese troops tried to calm down the populace around Lhasa until directions came from Beijing. It was clear that the relations between the Chinese government and the cooperative Tibetan civil government were definitively altered by the flight of the Dalai Lama.

The young pair enters a courtyard of the Zhaibung monastery, sitting on a slope overlooking the valley of Lhasa. This monastery was built in 1415 to symbolize prosperity. As one of three major monasteries near Lhasa, Zhaibung's annual festival gathered tens of thousands of people. Pasang wondered how the monastery held together after rain and snow during so many centuries. Earthquakes had knocked down some walls but the buildings made of rock and held together only by adobe remained.

The two pass through a large doorway that cannot be closed for religious reasons. Under the many trees in the courtyard, young students sat in circles. They took turns asking each other questions, to which the challenged student must answer by reciting memorized verses of ancient texts. Failure to respond properly brought laughs and ridicule from fellow students. Pasang was impressed but he asks his friend what good came from all this. Tao replied, "We must learn all these verses because of the truths they hold. Most of us do not read, so these verses have been passed on for centuries in this manner. Besides, this activity builds our power to concentrate as well as to learn."

"Learn what? Pasang asks. "Daily we see more Chinese troops come into the valley and we must learn what to do about this invasion. If you resist you are put into gangs of workers cutting down slopes to build a road in from southern China down below. Have you seen some of this? Even children are breaking up rocks to pave the road. Their pay is next to nothing. What do we do about this?" Tao replied, " Yes, I have seen much of this, but these things do not really matter. We show our true nature by enduring and surviving. Certainly, not resisting is wiser, for resisting only provokes more abuse." Pasang listens to Tao with a scornful attitude.

An older monk has been overhearing the conversation. He walks up to the friends and asks for the name of the young visitor. The old monk says, "We need more students here. Most of us are old and more young blood must train to carry on after us. Do you wish to join us?" Out of respect for the old man with the kindest eyes that Pasang has ever seen, he says nothing. "Come with me," the old monk says in a solemn voice, and the two young men follow. They enter a huge room with a high ceiling. The walls chipping off due to the passage of time, are covered with faded religious paintings. Tattered flags of many colors were draped everywhere and in the far end of the hall countless dusty scrolls nestle in holes in the wall. A hundred monks were kneeling as they chanted prayers over and over in unison. A huge drum with a low tone kept everything in rhythm. Pungent aromas filled the air in the hot room. Some of the smells were from incense, but the rest came from the fact that no one there seemed ever to have bathed. All this was a wonder to behold for Pasang. It was another world.

The old monk saw Pasang's reaction and let the surroundings soak into the young man. Certainly he thought all this would make Pasang more receptive to the monk's invitation. The three left the hall and walked out to a balcony overlooking the valley. Tao says nothing as the monk begins to ask Pasang about his background and how he feels about what is going on down below them. Pasang pours out his bitter feelings about the Chinese occupation. He is particularly angry at the passivity with which Tibetans accept the new masters. The monk saw his opening and said solemnly, "Everyone we see like ants far below us will pass away before long. What will be accomplished or remain from their labor and feelings? Anger will last no longer than love, and it will have accomplished little more. Each one of us is master of our feelings and no one else can shape our feelings unless we let them." The monk went on to describe the teachings of the master Buddha. Pasang paid close attention to the monk's words, for no one else had ever spoken to him in this way. Not even his father spoke of such things. His father spoke only about everyday, immediate things that must be done and how to do them. A personal relationship like this was not part of Pasang's childhood experience. Tao just watched and listened too. He hoped that his friend would become interested in the life of a monk. Pasang bowed towards the monk and begged that he must leave, for his father would be angry if he was late to help with household chores. Tao and the monk took their leave as well. Pasang strolled down the hill along narrow trails that turned back and forth due to the steep slope, leaving the monastery atop the mountain partly clouded by mist.

At the valley floor he was forced to jump into a ditch as Chinese troops marched by. The sight of the Chinese washed away the warm feelings he'd gained on the balcony far above. He was back in his own real world.

His monk friend sought him out a few days later and they went to the monastery again. The old monk was waiting for them. Pasang looked at him more closely than before. His face was dark and covered with countless wrinkles. The harsh climate and ruthless sun at this high elevation aged everyone's appearance. Pasang passed his hand over his own face and it was almost as smooth as Indus. Pasang accepted the monk's invitation to talk about the meaning of life and membership in the family of monks.

The monk began a long conversation about things and ideas Pasang wondered about but did not understand. " We are several hundred trapas living here like me," the monk said. "All of us are preparing for our next life during the time we pass in this gompa." Pasang asked, " Are there many gompas in Tibet?" The monk smiled and told him that there are about 6,000 gompas in Tibet. "Some are large with several thousand trapas, while others are small and contain only mud huts in miserable surroundings. The larger gompas oversee the many peasants living close to them. These support the gompas with their offerings of food and material things needed so that the trapas are free to study and meditate." Pasang asked about what the monks did in return for offerings by the people, although he knew part of the answer.

The old monk smiled at the mercenary question and went on to point out that every conscious act we perform affects our fate in the next life. Therefore sharing our goods is meritorious, as is helping someone or giving correct directions to a voyager. Since many Tibetans take weeklong long treks during a pilgrimage, they are likely to need directions from local people. The monk reminded Pasang that everyone appears to die, but in fact goes on to another existence. With the recitations of a trapa who has reached a level of virtue like a lama, a dying person can be directed to a better rebirth. A lama, for example, could make recitations, often loud and repetitive, to help the dying person reach the Land of Bliss. Pasang interjected that he had been told everyone had paternal and maternal gods that look out for one. "Yes," the old monk agreed, "but we need more help than our parent's gods can give us. To reach the paradise of Shambala on Earth, prayers and much meditation are necessary." The monk went on to explain how through prayer and meditation one can overcome the conditions of our body. We can control pain, fear, and hunger. We can simply will them to disappear.

Pasang was fascinated by all this wisdom. "You see," the monk now pronounced, "The Goddess of Mercy dwells in the giant Potala Palace, where the Dalai Lama lives. The God Chenrezi is incarnated in the Dalai Lama so that he will have great powers a soon as he completes his studies and is crowned by the senior lamas." Pasang said he was told the Dalai Lama was still doing his studies, even if he was in refuge somewhere in India. "Yes," the monk said. "The Dalai Lama was identified at the age of two, and he is now 12 years. To take his final examinations and be crowned he must be in Tibet, however." As it turned out, the Dalai Lama reached full status at the age of eighteen after returning to Tibet.

After a daylong session with the old monk, his friend Tao asked Pasang what he thought about all he had learned. "I don't know what to say because all of this is new to me. I am confused. Not all of these teachings make sense. For example, what do we do about the Chinese? They are setting up another government with a council of elders to govern in the place of the Dalai Lama. Most nobles are cooperating with the invaders to preserve their privileges, properties, and peasants. Our small army is helpless with the poor weapons the English have given us over time. Looking out for themselves, our officer ranks work with the Chinese to maintain control!" Listening to Pasang, Tao realized that his childhood friend needed time to think about becoming a novice trapa like himself.

Pasang was too involved with his feelings of patriotism. These feelings were mostly resentment at the foreigners, since nationalism as such did not exist yet in Tibet. Very few foreigners ever came to Tibet and they did not stay long because they were not welcome. Most Tibetans never saw someone different in their lifetime. The largely peaceful Chinese occupation was creating a new feeling of Tibetan nationalism. Pasang embodied that new feeling.

Pasang did not appear at the stream where Indus washed cloths daily. After several days she became worried because Pasang was very reliable. She inquired about him through her friends who lived near his village. She was not free to go to where Pasang lived, as her life followed a strict pattern close to her master's house. She learned that Pasang had left unexpectedly on a journey that would take him away for many weeks. She was worried because she knew these caravan trips could be dangerous among strange people and through difficult terrain.

Pasang's master was in a bad mood for whatever reason and he made his workers suffer for it by verbal abuse. This was not out of the ordinary. Because of the master's abusive treatment one of his herders became ill and could not join the men to herd beasts to the salt fields. The only medicine for the sick worker was for him to meditate day and night to regain his health. He mumbled prayers over and over, but he got worse. His fever left him unable to speak coherently. Meanwhile, the herdsmen were packing the yaks with supplies for the journey. The young man died in an adobe shack that served as a home for his small family. No one knew why he died. His family just muttered that his death was the will of the gods. The master looked around for a replacement and picked Pasang. Although he was young, the master knew that Pasang was very able with yaks. He conversed with the yaks and they obeyed as if they understood. There was no other choice available, even though most of the men were unhappy with relying on a boy for a man's job.

The crew organized the caravan as Pasang worried that

he could not meet Indus. He wanted to let her know about his coming absence on his own. Otherwise she would learn about what happened because of gossip among the village women. Everyone in the village knew about whatever happened. Such caravans involved numerous families and were vital to the people. Pasang was excited about the trip because his father was part of the caravan. Along the way he would teach Pasang many things about caravan work. On the trip the youth would learn that it was his father who had pleaded for his inclusion despite his youth.

Every night the group camped out in the open with millions of blinking stars above them. Their food was simple, cooked over a fire made from yak dung gathered along the trail. The smell of yak dung burning was very strong, as were the human aromas. No one bathed and daily sweat piled on top of yesterday's. Everyone was accustomed to this and neither did they notice that no one was good looking. The brutal sun at this altitude burnt everyone's faces so that they looked years older. Their food was partly to blame for their looks. Tsampa was Tibetan staple made of barley flour and yak butter hand mixed into a paste. That was the basic diet for most Tibetans. It was the Chinese that introduced varieties of vegetables like cabbages, turnips, and fruits into the Tibetan diet. The Chinese liked apples because they kept so well.

Over the campfire the men told stories along with traditional religious tales. These stories contained moral lessons. There were gods for everything; rivers, the sky, food, and harvests each had a god. Buddha, of course, was the most important. But the teachings of Buddha left most events up to humans to determine. Buddha did not decide human affairs. Personal decisions everyday were vital because they were an opportunity to earn karma. This good will in the eyes of Buddha helped determine into what form of life one would incarnate in one's next life. A fund of karma or good will could be gathered over time. Pasang listened to all this and accepted it as true. As he lay back and looked at the stars, he knew that his place in life was to believe and obey, so he just listened while the men talked around the fire late into the night. His thoughts were on

Indus.

Coming around a hill on the rocky trail they confronted another caravan. These were tough looking men. They were Indians and probably smugglers because they had weapons. Traditional hospitality led the two groups to camp near each other. In that manner they could keep an eye on each other. In the wilderness, merchants sometimes became bandits if they saw you were a suitable victim. Rarely was violence involved due to Buddhist respect for all life, but victims could be relieved of their goods before being allowed to resume their trek.

The leader of the smugglers was scary. Scars on his face were probably the result of hand-to-hand combat. The scary one dominated the conversation over the campfire. Pasang's group just listened politely while discreatly keeping track of all movements made by the smugglers. Pasang was fixed on the ugly one's face, taking in every word he said. The storyteller took note of the boy's interest in him. Pasang's eyes opened to a world he knew nothing about. The stories helped him understand what his people believed and how they behaved. Smugglers were an essential part of life in the mountainous regions. These men lived among the peoples of Tibet, Nepal and India. They moved goods that everyone needed, avoiding taxes where possible. Bribes for officials and occasional violence were necessary in this commerce.

Pasang offended the ugly smuggler by staring at his face. The dancing light of the campfire accentuated the scars. Noting the boy's curiosity, the ugly one told Pasang how he got the scars for which he was proud. Several years before, he went on to say, Indians were trying to gain independence from England. Her empire stretched around the globe but England always wanted more. England had agents in Tibet to scout conditions there in view of China's interest in the vast region. The border between Tibet and India was undefined in many places due to the terrain. A small lawyer trained in English law was leading a crusade for Indian independence. Mahatma Gandhi was leading unique nonviolent protests against English rule. Thousands marched in Indian cities and boycotted English imports to hurt England commercially. Stories about all this seemed to come from another world to Pasang.

England's hands were tied by its innate sense of fair play, which it evenly implemented with foreigners from time to time. England knew how to deal with violence. It had much practice at that, but nonviolence by many thousands was confusing. Moreover, Indian economic boycotts hurt English exporters. While parliament debated the course to take in India, England was arming some Indians to seize portions of Tibet. Indians went along with this military effort because they believed Tibet was rightly theirs anyway. Not only was Buddhism taken to Tibet from India, but India had also exercised much commercial influence there over centuries.

Tibetans resisted the Indian incursions but there was little they could do. Fortunately for them the English rifles given to the Indians were old and unreliable, like those the English sold to Tibetans. Some Tibetans cooperated with the Indians for certain reasons beyond commercial opportunism. The Tibetans feared Chinese claims over Tibet and they figured that Indians could be used against Chinese ambitions. Aristocratic Tibetan families and some of the monasteries differed over whose domination to accept. Most Tibetans just wanted to be free of any strangers.

Pasang finally heard the ugly man's name when a smuggler called out to him. Torfu, the leader, expressed annoyance at the interruption and continued to talk around the fire about regional affairs, but now he was talking mostly to Pasang. Torfu was reminded of his own youth when he was slender and had a smooth face like Pasang's. The men just listened politely to their leader because they had already heard the stories that were so important to him. The Tibetans just listened while keeping track of the smugglers to avoid any surprise.

Torfu had come to hate everyone. The English, Chinese, and the Tibetans were all objects of his scorn for different reasons. His youth had been wasted on patriotism and now he just made money, trading outside of the law when necessary. Sometimes his group was forced to fight policemen and other bandits. Trade in the Himalayas was still a hazardous occupation.

Pasang's father died suddenly a few days later from injuries when a heavy load slipped off a yak and fell on him. No one could help him as internal injuries ended his life with little suffering. The two groups parted, and according to custom, left the father out in the open for birds to eat away. Torfu had come to like Pasang, and so out of pity he told him that one of his men would take care of the body. This involved cutting up the father into small pieces. In this manner, as food for birds of prey, he would re-join nature. The birds seemed to know what was happening as their numbers grew in the sky above waiting for the men to leave.

The Tibetan caravan resumed its march towards the salt fields far off on the high and barren plateau. The salt from these fields was a very salable product. From the distance Pasang could barely see the Nepalese man working on his father for birds to take away. Pasang was sad and alone now. He must hold his weight with the herders in his group that would not tolerate his youth now that his father could not speak for him. He compared his situation with that of Indus, now living in the house of Chang.

In the arid plain the Tibetans gathered salt rocks which the yaks carried to towns scattered around Tibet. Actually, there were no markers for the regions or national borders. Language and customs were more important than nationality. Tibetans simply knew each other because of their language, religion, and customs of the region where they lived. These were what comprised being Tibetan. After several days the group marched over frightening mountain passes. As they reached a summit, they customarily shouted out " Lha gyalo" (The Gods win, the demons are defeated!). In some places summer heat could cause drifts of snow to come smashing down over the trail.

The sales of salt went well. Pasang looked closely at people of lower elevations who were new to him. The people in these towns ate strange foods and dressed differently. Pasang thought they were good looking. These people relied on Tibetans for salt. They feared traveling high into mountainous regions and simply traded iron goods and some finished products from India in return for salt. Pasang noticed everything the traders did very closely and everything that happened. The Tibetan herdsmen got drunk and most went into shacks with local women. Indus was always on Pasang's mind and so he was repelled by the thought of doing the same. Besides, these women were not Tibetan and were adults. He was actually a little afraid of being with one of these local women. He just walked away as some of them made sexual gestures enticing him to enter their huts.

After several days in the last town, the Tibetans organized the herd for the trip back to Tibet. This would involve going up mountain ranges in late summer. Trees were starting to turn and before long no more trees were in sight because they were too high for them to grow. Nights were turning colder; this weather was familiar to them. Their spirits improved as the weather changed, since they were going home.

Two days into the trek uphill, the ground shook, moving back and forth. Earthquakes were familiar to them. The yaks scattered and it took much work to gather them. After gathering the yaks the Tibetans noticed that a landslide had covered the narrow passage ahead. This was the only trail back, as far as they knew. Pasang could not imagine then that the group would have to wait until next spring before resuming their return. At least they were alive. Soon after the earthquake, snow began to fall higher up. The men argued over whose fault it was that they delayed the return for several weeks. There was nothing to do but make arrangements to camp outside a village. As it turned out, they would have to wait there until snows melted in spring and a new trail could be found around the avalanche.

So much time went by that the families back in Tibet wondered what had happened to their group. Was some mountain god taking revenge for offenses committed against it? Such beliefs were common. Over the years some caravans were never heard of again. That was part of life in Tibet. Pasang matured much during this time away from home and Indus.

So too did Indus mature back home within sight of the beautiful Potala Palace. Dalai Lamas had lived there with hundreds of monks and lamas for many centuries. At the beginning a Tibetan king had started the construction of this huge structure out of love for his wife. In time the Potala structure contained a thousand rooms with chapels of all sizes. It came to be one of the outstanding buildings in the world.

Indus knew little about religion at her age. Indeed, girls got no education at all in Tibet. Older women taught the workings of religion to their young. These knew only what they had been taught to do. Indus, like everyone else, spun prayer wheels as she would pass by a temple. These prayer wheels were always spinning because there were always people passing by. There were many monasteries in the valley. Their monks of various ages trudged into towns seeking donations. Along the same paths pilgrims from far away also trudged to visit holy sites, thus gaining karma.

When Pasang's caravan finally returned and entered the valley in central Tibet, snowmelt had swelled the rivers and so their passage was slow and hazardous. The men found that many things were different in just one year. The caravan passed numerous demolished monasteries. Earthquakes had not done the damage. This was human destruction. More so than before, monks could be seen begging for food, while other monks were working at a job. They were no longer just praying or studying in the monasteries as they had done for as long as anyone could remember. The monks were now homeless. Since Tibetans were obliged to support the monks to earn karma. Pasang's caravan helped monks as much as it could on the way back. Gradually they learned about what had happened since they left.

Chinese troops were patrolling the trails toward Lhasa. The military patrols were heavily armed and did not speak Tibetan. The caravan communicated by signs and the Chinese by sharp commands. After examining the cargo for weapons the caravan was permitted to proceed. Not until they were out of hearing range did the men talk about the events with great emotion. These conditions were not like anything anyone had ever seen. At several locations one could see hundreds of people digging away for a roadbed. Some were on their knees pounding on rocks to make piles of grading material. Others gathered mounds of fist-size rocks to carry away as foundation for a paved road. Everything was being done by hand. This road was along the main route to Lhasa, a walking trail for people and yaks. Every so often Chinese troops would appear suddenly, as if they had been hiding and jumped out at the last minute.

Pasang and the men arrived at the land owned by their master. He was not there. Amidst great confusion due to Chinese directions, the master's workers were now setting the boundaries for their own plots of land. The workers told the caravan that this owner, like many hundreds of others, lost his land. The former peasants each were now in possession of a small plot of land roughly equal in size. They had a paper they could not read, establishing ownership of their own land for the first time. Their former master had the same amount of land as everyone else. Within months the Chinese occupiers had ended centuries of feudalism. To a man, former peasants were delighted with these changes brought about by the Chinese. Moreover, their former masters were being humbled and this made them happy. Living next to parcels of their neighbors on a basis of equality was new and exciting.

Gunshots pierced the clean air now and then. Some owners

who interfered with land distribution were shot on the spot. So too were monks who interfered with dismantling of monasteries. Compliant monks were put to work on roads and other public works. The monks and nuns were free to earn a living any way they could. Many were frightened by the new freedom and the hazards of being self-sufficient.

Pasang found his family and related the death of his father. After tending to family affairs that were now his to attend to he set off to find Indus. Indus was overjoyed to see him, but both had to restrain displaying their emotions in public. In just one year Indus had blossomed into a lovely young woman. Pasang could only look at her, but could not spin her around in his arms.

Just before the Chinese arrived from below the eastern regions of Tibet, she had been sold to the old man who had been chasing her by the stream. He was wealthy before the Chinese came. Now he had no more land than any of his former serfs. But like other members of the Tibetan upper class he was finding ways to do business with the Chinese occupiers. These were trying to win over the Tibetans with persuasion and benefits like land distribution. Chinese political policy called for all peasants to have land of their own to care for their family. Chairman Mao Zedong himself had said, "Changes must come slowly". Indus's new owner, Chang, was scheming how to offer his managerial services to the Chinese to regain his prominence. The Chinese recognized his value and planned to use his abilities at the start. Later, time would tell what long term value he had for the Chinese.

The encounters between the lovers were few and only in public to avoid problems. Pasang was both glad and sad to see Indus since they had little time to talk together. On one occasion, as they passed each other, she told him not to worry. She still loved only him. As it turned out, the old man was too old to have sex with her. She was simply an ornament for him. Chang, like many other shrewd Tibetans, was becoming successful helping the Chinese organize a new society. Most Tibetans were simply passive in the face of overwhelming power that brought mixed blessings.

Confusion was rampant in all walks of life. The Dalai Lama was in a curious position. The Chinese respected his religious role for the time being. They believed that most traces of the theocracy would gradually pass away in the face of their new regime. The Chinese harassed Buddhist activities and ridiculed religion publicly in a variety of ways- on radio, with publications and on television, which they introduced in Lhasa. Indeed, the television station was multistory and only slightly smaller than the communist party headquarters. Secular governmental institutions were starting to replace religious practices and social customs that had regulated public conduct for centuries.

All military and civil authority was in Chinese hands. However, Tibetan groups were organized to give a substance to Tibetan semi-autonomy. For example, never before had ordinary people been involved in gathering census data, regulating land distribution, and other such matters of public life. A Tibetan-wide council was organized, comprised of cooperating Tibetans. The Dalai Lama accepted the role of the council to manage secular affairs, since his religious authority was not being challenged. Under instructions from Chairman Mao himself, Chinese policy held that gradualism and benefits for the Tibetan masses would win over Tibetans to communism.

Chinese assigned as immigrants were coming to Tibet as pioneers in order to promote the blending of the two peoples. These immigrants were only of the Han ethnic group. however. China was composed of about fifty five ethnic groups with their own customs and dialects. Indeed, holding the People's Republic of China together was a source of constant concern for the communist party. In the far west of China its Arabic population was Islamic and resented Chinese control. The government in Beijing wanted to fully absorb Tibet and so its Chinese immigrants were of the dominant Han ethnic group to establish its culture there. The Chinese coming to Tibet got the better jobs and benefits, like new housing. A new dominant ethnic group was emerging in social and economic life, not only in political control.

Gradually the Chinese proceeded to modernize all aspects of life in Tibet. Some changes were welcomed, while others were resisted because these broke down traditional relationships. Posters ridiculed religion and monks got scant respect from Chinese. They were ridiculed as oppressors, since they sought alms, rather than work. Some Chinese opened stores where many new gadgets and supplies were available.

An ever-larger number of urban Tibetans were now employed and with their meager wages were joining an emerging commercial economy. Social standing stemming from a monetary position gradually overwhelmed the older source of social standing. Opposition to Chinese authority and the Han grew gradually in spite of what appeared like social progress. Fighting by Tibetan partisans broke out here and there in an irregular manner. However, resistance to the Chinese was less all the time. There was no central direction for Tibetan resistance to the Chinese. The Dalai Lama did not counsel or support armed resistance. In the early years of Chinese incorporation of Tibet, the occupiers made every effort to avoid military responses to Tibetan resistance. This initial policy shaped in Beijing was soon set aside in view of its failure to overcome Tibetan resistance. The gradual changes Chairman Mao called for brought some benefits, but not a general change in attitude. Tibetans resented Chinese domination in spite of the benefits.

Pasang became one of the Tibetan patriots. He met with others and they planned ways to disrupt Chinese control. Some Tibetans disclosed their identity to Chinese authorities in return for favors. The Chinese gradually rounded up young men like Pasang. Their fate was hard labor on road building or tearing down monasteries. Untold numbers of troublemakers simply disappeared.

There was no escape from the Chinese troops once they had

your name. New Chinese programs like public education, medical services and employment made it easier to keep track of everyone. Pasang decides to flee when he learns that young men like him are being rounded up. But first he must see Indus. They manage to steal away to the place where they first met. She is a grown woman now, beautiful to him in every way. They make love close to the stream where they would meet to talk. This is so special to him. Indus tells him her owner was too old for love, he just fondled and looked at her before he went to sleep. Chang was understandably tired at night after a day making money cooperating with the Chinese. For a fee from the authorities he gathered Tibetan workers for construction work. Chang got payment from the Chinese contractors and kickbacks from the workers, as well. Getting older bothered him mainly because he had less time left to get richer. In some ways he was better off than in the old days when he was a lord over his peasants. Now he earned money at every turn without any responsibility for his serfs.

Pasang hears they are looking for him and there is no time to delay running away. He tells Indus he is leaving that very night, but he cannot take her along because of the dangers involved. She tries everything she can think of but cannot persuade him to stay. She insists that the Chinese are doing more good than harm. Some things are changing for the better, she pleads. He will not accept this. They avoid arguing due to the sorrow of his departure. She promises to wait for him no matter what, and he promises to return to her no matter what.

Soon after Pasang fled she realized that she was pregnant. She was so happy and vowed solemnly to do anything to provide for their child as she stroked her belly. Her master customarily hung a small rag as a flag over the door of the woman he wanted that night. Indus had been passed over for some time because she was indifferent to him. The other two women watched their door every evening to see whose turn it was to please their master. In view of her situation, Indus ignored the flag over another's door. Her sessions with Chang had been incomplete before, but now she pretended passion. Chang gladly took advantage of her change of heart. Her affection brought him to completion, to his happy surprise. In a short time Chang was delighted. He would now have an heir to his estate and proof that he was still virile.

In time a boy is born. Indus tries to make her master happy for the benefit of her baby. Love for Pasang and their child brings her to behave affectionately with her master all the time. Fortunately for Indus her master is busy working with the Chinese so he makes few demands on her. He is becoming important politically, making money constantly. At night Indus found a new way to please her master. She sang old peasant songs. Her lovely voice put him to sleep before he thought of making love. How could he imagine she was thinking of Pasang as she sang affectionately to him? Everything she did was for Pasang and their child.

Before long the boy starts to sit up without rolling over, then he crawls and finally walks. Indus sees Pasang in everything he does and in her eyes he looks just like Pasang. Chang is unaware of all this. The other two women in Chang's household still resent Indus, but they can't help loving the little boy as he grows up. Ola, the older one, unlike the other, genuinely loves her master and she wants him to be happy in bed with Indus, if no longer with her. She suggests to Indus how to please a man. Ola's good will is teaching her even more - the lessons of unselfish love. Indus is thinking about Pasang as she learns about things to do with a man. She had not done any of these things with Pasang. Ola's love for her master made her willing to teach Indus many little things, often laughing as she thought of her master's pleasure with his new toy.

Lhasa in the 1950s

CHAPTER TWO
Fleeing To Nepal

The next morning Pasang awakens from his freezing night in the mountain pass where the smugglers had left him to die. He has some frostbite on his toes, which will stay with him thereafter. He recalls the powers of meditation he was taught by the old monk at the monastery. Maybe other things he heard might be true as well. He finds his way along the narrow mountain trail. The smugglers he had joined were up ahead, to his surprise. They had been delayed, moving aside snow and rocks so that their yaks could proceed towards the Dokar Pass into Nepal. Torfu is glad to see Pasang. It had been with mixed feelings that he ordered his group to move on when Pasang had fallen off the trail the day before. As the group came over the Himalayan crest they all gave out with the customary yells, "The Gods win. The demons are defeated!" The yells carried far across the mountain pass and the echoes came back as if to let everyone know.

Walking becomes easier as they trek down into the beautiful Kathmandu valley. All this was familiar to the others, but it was a wonder to Pasang. Down at 4,000 feet everything was green. Large trees were everywhere, not like in Tibet. Still farther down, flowers were scattered along streams, giving off pleasant fragances. One of Torfu's group explains that various herbs from this region make for good trade back in Tibet and India, not far away. This group, like many others, travels all over this region for trade and mischief, whatever suits the occasion.

Some pilgrims cross their path. These arjopas travel in small groups from one holy site to another. They come from far away at times, living off the land and charity. For the sake of karma people gave them alms and just hoped they would move along. Nepalese was another language, and in some parts of Nepal, Tibetan and Indian influences made communication difficult. Pasang noted that the young girls were pretty. The Yanus had olive toned, smooth skin. They reminded him of Indus. However, unlike in Tibet, adults did not have many wrinkles on their faces. The children running about all looked healthy and happy.

Some officials came by on patrol and made inquiries of Pasang's group. Torfu spoke for them. The Nepalese were careful with Tibetans because some could make problems with China. Nepal was caught between two competing giants and made efforts to not offend them. Borders of the three had been sources of friction over many centuries. China's occupation of Tibet made for increased sensitivity among the Himalayan giants, so small Nepal took care not to offend either major power. Tibetan refugees were a nuisance to Nepal.

Torfu explained to Pasang that Nepal was a monarchy, whose young king, Birendra, was educated in America. The young monarch was busy ordering many new things for the kingdom. Roads were being expanded and old ones improved. Trees were being planted to repair deforestation and wild flowers seeded everywhere. In many respects the valley of Kathmandu was like a garden compared to Tibet.

Efforts by the king to stop the production and traffic in hashish, marijuana, and heroin were a mixed success. Indians who sought the drugs always found sellers, although the traffic was banned. Nepalese heroin made with sugar was popular in

India. Nepalese tea of many varieties was also sought abroad. The Harvard-educated king was clearly trying to make his kingdom a sort of Shangri-la in modern times.

Gradually Pasang learned about Nepalese culture. He learned the words for greetings, " I salute the god within you," and other essential phrases. A stray Nepali mastiff puppy took to Pasang, which pleased him. Stray dogs were not common in Tibet before the Chinese took over. After their arrival the Chinese gave coins to anyone that killed dogs, cats, and any other loose creature. A companion told him that mastiffs grew enormous. Pasang had no way to care for him, so he frightened the puppy away. Torfu's group was always on the move anyway, so dog care was not possible.

The gang left Kathmandu to take Nepalese spices to India where they were prized. Torfu and his companions got along well with the people en route, although they were a mixture of Hindus, Buddhists, and other groups like Animists. The Tibetans were respectful of everyone. They were aware that Indians recruited fierce Nepali Gurkha to serve in their military. So too the English had employed Gurkhas since colonial times. The Tibetans acted like guests in the complex region. They avoided difficulties by being friendly with everyone to assure their own safety among strangers.

Pasang stayed behind from one trading expedition to India and figured he would live off his share from previous trips the group had made. By 1959 when he fled Lhasa some 10,000 other Tibetans had found refuge in Nepal. They encountered some hostility as locals learned they were not tourists but refugees. They competed for work and asked for help as was common in Tibet. Tibetans streamed in despite Chinese efforts to cut them off at mountain passes. With some money the border guards could be induced to look the other way. Besides, many border guards were Tibetans now cooperating with the new regime. After all, so too was the Dalai Lama cooperating with the Chinese.

One afternoon Pasang stopped near a wall to urinate where

he wanted to, as Tibetans were prone to do. He felt relieved and sat down against the wall in the warm sunshine. With eyes closed thinking of Indus he stroked his full erection. A Nepalese woman walked by and stopped to watch him give himself pleasure. She just stood there with a smile on her face. Pasang finished and sat with eyes still closed, wishing Indus was with him in this lovely place.

He opened his eyes and saw the woman standing there looking at him. Somewhat startled, he didn't know what to do. A sharp breeze arose and it pressed her loose tunic against her body. The silky cloth left little to hide. From where Pasang was sitting he was right across her thighs and looking up. His gaze traveled from her thighs just in front of him, up to her full breasts and aroused nipples. She took notice of his fascination but said nothing until he stood up somewhat awkwardly. The whole episode lasted only a minute.

Tara was an adult woman on the younger side. Tall and slender, she was confident of herself, as Pasang would soon learn. He agreed to her request to help her move some things that were too heavy for her. The job was nearby, she said. In fact the two were just outside her home inside the wall where he had sat down to please himself. Pasang gathered himself and meekly followed her into the yard.

A lovely garden surrounded her home, with flowers and aromatic bushes under flowering trees, the likes of which Pasang had never seen.

He moved some heavy pots to where she wanted and was sweating. She offered him some food and he gladly accepted the offer. He was starved, actually. As they went into her house she muttered some instructions to a servant, as the two proceeded into a room to eat. Pasang had never been in a house, as such. Tibetans like him lived in mud plastered adobe huts. They lived, ate around a fire, and slept on a wool blanket spread on the dirt floor. Their huts were neat but utterly frugal. This house had furniture, hanging tapestries and windows. The meat was a delight, for rarely had he any meat to eat. So too the vegetables and fruit were a delight. She offered him some warm tea. He had no way knowing he was having his first cannabis blended with tea.

Tara could speak Tibetan. She was broadly educated, as he would soon learn. Tara led him into another room where two servants were waiting over a steaming basin. By this time Pasang was so overwhelmed by everything that he acceded to Tara's offer of a bath. Two women pulled off his dirty clothing for washing and proceeded to scrub him all over with balls of grass so thoroughly and vigorously that it hurt. He had never bathed and there was much for the women to scrub off. The hot water was scented and soon he was relaxed and getting sleepy. The women were not affected by his nakedness. They gave him a tunic and led him into another room. Tara was waiting for him there.

She began a long conversation, telling him about herself and how she lived. She told him she was shorthanded growing herbs and medicines. Figuring there must be a man in the house, he asked about her husband. Her husband had died that year, she said, and she went on about the fertile ground that produced three crops per year of some plants, and how the crops required regular attention. Agents came for her teas from as far as India, although most of the tea was for local consumption. Watering, weeding, pruning, and drying of the herbs was a full time job. All this was fascinating to Pasang and he listened attentively. A full stomach, warm bath, and the cannabis tea took their toll. Tara led him to a bedroom where he almost fell onto the bed, and he dropped off to sleep. Tara looked at him a long time and then lay down alongside.

When Pasang awoke he felt her arm embracing him. He didn't move while he tried to understand the situation. Her perfume was delightful and he could feel her body warmth. He thought of Indus and wished she were there. This went on for a short while as the sunlight came through the window. Pasang did not know what to do.

Tara moved a bit and so Pasang turned over to face her. He didn't know what to expect. She looked so rested and beautiful. Making love sprang to his mind. Before he could become aroused, she simply greeted him in Tibetan and slid off the bed. In a matter of fact way she said, " I have chores to do in town. Would you accompany me? I will acquaint you with parts of the city. It is quite large, you know."

Tara's house was at the end of a paved road leading to the city of Kathmandu. In the opposite direction the rustic countryside stretched out as far as the eye could see. All around one could see high mountains, covered with eternal snow, and to the north the ranges leading to Mount Everest itself, the highest mountain in the world. On the other side of this enormous range there was Tibet and his beloved Indus. As the pair walked towards the city, Pasang took note of the small houses, farm plots, and corrals for animals, especially cattle, sheep, and goats. He figured all these would taste good since in Tibet stock was scarce and expensive for lack of grass. Sturdy work animals like yaks were eaten for food after they could not carry their weight or breed any longer. Meat was not common in the Tibetan diet and so all this stock made him like Nepal. He got the impression that individual families lived in the small homes, with their land and animals around them. These people did not look like someone's peasants; they seemed to be living on their own. In Tibet almost everyone belonged to the owner of the land they were born on. Only the nomads were free.

Tara enjoyed playing the role of tourist guide. They walked alongside each other, rather than he ahead of her as in Tibet. They drew nearer to the city and encountered small shops selling numerous things for everyday living. He stopped short. He heard music from a radio, which he had never seen before. The music was Tibetan, no less. Tara was amused and pointed out that shops played music so passers by would be enticed to enter and buy. As for the music being Tibetan, she said that Indian and European music were also common, and even American jazz. He had never heard American music. Glenn Miller's band was blaring out of another shop down the road. This was another world. What was he doing here, he wondered?

Tourists to Nepal numbered many thousands coming from everywhere. Lately most tourists came from China now that many Chinese had money to travel. Mountain climbing was popular among tourists, and had become somewhat of an industry. Tibetans were indispensable guides and carriers. Mountains for them were mainly obstacles. Now they were a source of employment. As Tara pointed up towards Mount Everest and the glaciers, a giant balloon drifted by. Tourists looked down from the balloon basket taking photos of the spectacular scenery.

Hunters for Yeti come every year, Tara pointed out. " I don't believe there is a Yeti, but its good for tourism. The searchers come from many countries and buy equipment and hire packers and guides. Some people call this creature the Abominable Snowman, part human or bear. Even Sir Edmund Hillary, who conquered Mt. Everest, led an expedition looking for the Yeti in 1960 to no avail. They found some suspicious tracks on a nearby glacier, nothing else."

King Birenda was opening up his country hidden high up between India and China. Travel by road had always been arduous and dangerous due to banditry. Nepal had been a well-kept secret over the centuries. A new airport opened in 1949 and so people with means came from around the globe to Kathmandu. Global mail service, and even television, as well as radio, were available in Kathmandu. Construction on all forms of infrastructure was underway. Bikas, or development projects, were common. Reforestation required many workers, as did construction on the East-West highway to link the entire nation. The royal thrust to modernize life in Nepal even included public information about maintaining health, as well as birth control. The young, Harvard-educated king was leaping over centuries to improve life in Nepal. Tibetan refugees were in the middle of all this. They found work with some Bika project or another. Tibetans were easy to spot because most extended their tongue to great one another, especially to greet someone that merited respect.

Spotting some Tibetan workers, Pasang asked Tara, "How come you speak Tibetan? " I speak Indian and Mandarin too. I was taking university studies when I got married," she said. Pasang took note of these remarks and wondered just who this woman was. So much about her was new to him. They walked on to where Pasang stopped short again. There was a TV screen in a shop to entertain pedestrians. Tara pointed out that it was showing a novella, a popular Indian drama series, full of drama and romance, and that ordinary people followed every episode, she pointed out. People came by at the right time and stood by on the sidewalk to see this next exciting episode. Although poor in dramatic quality, the series expanded public awareness of the world beyond their narrow experience.

Farther along their trek of narrow streets Tara entered a teashop for a rest. The proprietor knew Tara and seated the two with great respect. By now nothing surprised Pasang. Tara pointed out as she sipped her tea that her husband was well known and the two had frequented the shop. Unlike in Tibet, Pasang noted that men and women spoke quite casually to each other in Nepal, like equals. Tara took time to have Pasang taste several tea flavors and asked for his opinion. Shops like this were customers for the teas on her land. Again Indus came to mind and Pasang wished she could share his company and the many teas. In other shops along the way he saw fabrics and dresses he wanted for Indus.

In the center of Kathmandu Tara went into a government office. Pasang followed along and noticed that the officials in charge knew Tara and extended cordial greetings. She went up to a counter and paid some money, then walked away with a receipt. She had paid for next year's tax to sell herbs. Now Pasang guessed why she stopped at teashops. She was keeping abreast of the market.

Around a corner they came to an impressive wall and large

gate. Just inside the gate some heavy trucks stood guard to keep out any unauthorized vehicles. This is the entrance to the royal palace, Tara told him. Pasang was distracted by some noises across the wide road and failed to see that the two guards stood up straighter when they recognized Tara and nodded in recognition. Tara pointed out that greater precautions were now being taken since some peasants were demanding greater reforms and threatened violent action. They called themselves Maoists, taking their inspiration from China. Their numbers were small, but growing. It seemed as if reforms in process only served to whet their appetite for more reforms.

The nobility posed a problem for the reformist king. He was familiar with the outside world, but the nobility was very provincial. The noble generations had been locked up in the mountain kingdom for about 4,000 years. King Birendra relied on the nobility as the backbone of the monarchy, but nobles only grudgingly accepted the reforms and modernization projects of the king. Maoists scoffed at the king's reforms, largely because these reforms made their demands less attractive. At the king's insistence Nepal was scheduled to have parliamentary elections to make the country a constitutional monarchy. Both the Maoists and the nobility opposed such a change, for their own reasons. All these events and political currents made an impression on Pasang because he related all these events to his homeland. Again, Indus was on his mind. How was she? What was she doing? He had no way of knowing she was tending to their son.

Tara could tell that all these things revealed a new world to Pasang. She took pleasure in educating him. He in turn was a rapid learner, as she would soon see. Newspapers and magazines were new to him, and he spent time looking at the pictures since he was illiterate. Pasang asked Tara what she thought about all the complicated politics bearing down on young King Birenda. " That would take quite a few cups of tea to tell you about," she said with a smile.

The shadows were getting long as they approached her house in the suburbs of Kathmandu. The moon had just climbed over the mountains, and it was full. The maid prepared a warm tub of scented water while the couple had a leisurely meal. Tara suggested he take a bath before retiring, but only after he enjoyed a special tea she had prepared. The maid took off his garments in a matter-of-fact way, and he submitted since there was no way predicting Nepalese customs. He soaked a bit and relaxed completely, smelling the aroma and thinking of Indus. The woman washed him thoroughly and then stroked his organ lightly, as she knew how to please him. He was already thinking of Indus as his erection arose. Since his eyes were closed he could not see that she too was smiling, enjoying her work.

Usually he awoke in the morning to feel Tara alongside with her arm wrapped softly around him. But that was all. He figured that she got up, dressed, and came into his bedroom to start the day in this manner. When he had made polite advances to signal lovemaking, Tara would put him off with a smile, and remark, "Not yet." However, tonight was to be different. The moon was full and so bright this high up that you could read a newspaper. Tara led Pasang into her own bedroom for the first time. He followed her like a little boy and lay down on his stomach as she wished. From his feet up she began to massage him. He was amazed at how much feeling he had on the bottom of his feet. She knew just where to press the bottom of his feet to make him feel good. The smell of the sweet, scented oil made it all even better. As he lay in sheer delight she began to tell him why she had asked him to wait two weeks for making love.

Tara went on to say that many centuries ago a Brahman priest in India developed a belief that sensual pleasure helped a person attain a spiritual condition of well-being like no other. Ordinary copulation without true love was what animals do, and indeed it was a distortion of what people were and what they could attain. Indian thinkers differed about these ideas over time but gradually a consensus emerged about the vital, spiritual energy involved in lovemaking. At the start, the secrets of these beliefs were meant for the nobility—they were far too good for ordinary people. Only after a long time did some of these ideas become a religion of sorts, and the secrets spread out to ordinary people.

As Tara worked her way up his spine she pointed out in whispers that sexual activity was one way of arousing awesome energy dormant at the base of the spine. This force can also be awakened by those trained in yoga exercises. The ability to control this energy could lead to moksa, a release from the cycle of life and death, the feelings are so intense. Pasang just listened to all this as he gradually slipped into complete relaxation in her hands. All the ideas about the seven invisible centers of vital energy in the body he could not understand, he simply felt better than ever before.

Ancient Chinese medicine and philosophy differed from Indian thought, she said. Chinese thought was deeper in some respects. They believed that there is a system of forces in nature-a form of natural order called Tao. Tao is a way to live harmoniously and master the human condition. Proper diet, personal care, and thought combine to maintain health and understanding about nature and people. Sex wisdom was one of the Tao concepts and activities. " How often should one enjoy physical pleasure?" he asked as he lay feeling good. "Well," she said, "there are no fixed rules, to my knowledge. My husband and I came to believe that nothing should be done too much, not even this." His grunts sounded like disbelief. "Look," she said, "tell me what is your favorite food. Would you still want more if you ate it all the time? You would soon grow tired of it and want a change. Is that not so? Anything is better when you build up an appetite for it. My husband and I decided to make love when the moon was full. That way, we would never get tired of making love. I would look up at night and count the nights until the moon was full again. Only then would we make love. That is why, Pasang, I told you not yet the other night." He said, " I am sure your husband became a moon watcher also."

"Is it not breaking the rule for me to wake up with your arm around me?" She said, "No, that is only affection." The moon was still high in the sky by the time she had worked her way up to his neck and head. Pasang was not in a state of Tao or bliss, because he was barely awake. Tara turned him over and started to massage him from the head down. She saved his huge erection for the last. She wet him well with her kisses and mounted him. She put him in position and slipped down, taking him deep inside. And so it went that night. They awoke the next morning, but this time in each other's arms.

As the months went by Pasang found himself looking up at the night sky. He counted the nights until full moon, but at least he woke up every morning with one warm arm around him to start the day. His happiness made him think constantly about how to earn money for a return to Tibet and Indus. Refugees from Tibet came by regularly. He could always spot them because most stuck out their tongue to greet one another. He learned about changes back home through their accounts. His longing for Indus was only increased, not diminished by his love for Tara. Sharing love with Tara did not diminish his longing for Indus, it only made it greater.

CHAPTER THREE
New Love

Chang was content under Chinese rule, much to his surprise. He had lost his lands and peasants, but he was earning good money as a labor contractor for the Chinese. Chang arranged for manual workers, and paid them with funds from the Chinese contractor. For his services he took a percent of their wages. The workers were happy, the Chinese projects advanced and Chang grew wealthier. It also pleased him to have special status among not only Tibetans but the Chinese as well. Everyone knew he was a trusted collaborator to Lieutenant Li.

Everyday his son grew and Indus made him happy. How could Chang ever imagine that in bed Indus was always thinking of someone else as he made love to her? Chang had a routine for lovemaking. He would disrobe her and lay her down on the bed. He liked to hold her face in his hands as if her face was a lovely flower. Then, starting with her face he would kiss and taste her with his tongue. All the while Indus would be thinking about Pasang because Chang's caresses were not truly welcome. Thanks to her successful concentration she wore a smile thinking of Pasang. Chang thought the smile was because of him and this made him happy.

One day Li came to the house on business with Chang. Indus served them tea. Li watched her as she went back and forth. Both Chang and Indus noticed that he looked at her with interest. It was customary for women always to look down and not into the eyes of a man. Indus looked right back at Li and he liked that. He liked her spirit and was attracted to her immediately. He liked her looks as well as her boldness. Chang noticed all this, and with resignation born of a survival instinct and ambition, he decided that whatever Li wanted with Indus was going to be fine with him.

Li came to the house one evening to look at Indus again, and found the Chang house in turmoil. Little Pasang was crying and everyone was chanting prayers in resignation. Indus was weeping as she held the little boy in her arms. In keeping with Buddhist beliefs, Tibetans believed that prayers and meditation, rather than medicines, would help resolve the child's fate. Li approached the child and, feeling his temperature, snatched him from the arms of Indus and stormed out to his car. Indus could barely catch up as Li's driver took them off to a local clinic. Li barked out orders to the Chinese nurses. They immediately diagnosed the problem well enough to give the boy an injection and give Indus some medicines for him to take at home. Li left for his office after taking the two back home. In bidding farewell to Li, Indus uttered the typical Tibetan prayer of thanks, "May all the Buddhas remain to protect the world from darkness." Li could not understand Tibetan well enough to understand the prayer, but that did not matter. In several days young Pasang was just fine. When Li next came to visit, Indus had another expression on her face. She looked at Li with love in her eyes. She would never forget that Li had saved her son's life.

In time Lt. Li talks to Indus about his work as they share a pillow. He is in charge of building part of the road from southern China up and over steep mountains into the valley of Lhasa. On the new road heavy trucks will bring up building materials for new construction projects, such as roads, hospitals, public buildings, and schools. He explains that the People's Republic wants Tibetan youth to be healthy and learn vocations, not just farming and herding. Under the new regime students will learn Mandarin because all instruction will be in the official Chinese language. By starting with the children, eventually everyone will speak the same language.

On another occasion the two take a stroll together as Li looks over government projects in process. They watch former monks working on a new road, chipping large rocks into gravel to pave a road beyond Lhasa. Li says he can't imagine how people got along without roads, using only trails to follow. The nation needs healthy and productive citizens, he tells her. Roads for trucks will help develop the country. Indus is learning to appreciate Li's work. During the next meeting he tells her that he must oversee building a hospital for the region. It will be modern and fully equipped, serving much of central Tibet. But she is not really listening, she is simply looking at him with affection in her eyes. He sees this and summarily leads her off to a nearby hut to make love on the straw. She tells Li not to worry about her owner because to please a Chinese official he will not question anything Li wants. Chang knows Indus meets with Li and is agreeable because this relationship will help him conduct more business with Li. She returns home after dark, because by this time of the year the days are short high up in the Himalayas.

Li tells Indus that she must liberate herself from her owner. Li understands Indus's situation in the house of Chang; he is her lord and master. He is like other Tibetan nobles. Chinese occupation has not changed old customs. These customs and religion held together a class system by which a few privileged families had their way with ordinary Tibetans. Although this society had been stable for countless centuries, it was the society Li and the Chinese were in Tibet to abolish.

With both their heads over a pillow, Li told Indus how he had grown up among Mongolian tribes free from a formal class structure. Strength, skill and leadership shaped social standing. Mongolians had chiefs chosen by family groups because they were natural leaders. Some family groups were small and others large. Families wandered in annual cycles across the endless grassy plains of Siberia. They traveled on horseback until they found good grazing for their cattle. At some spot a family would set up their fur- covered huts and stay as long as the grazing held out. Other families might be camped a short distance away, all relating to each other as equals. Hostilities arose from time to time, but clan groups tended to live with respect for each other. Among these people, known for their native ferocity, it was most unwise to brovoke hostilities as these lasted a long time. Many Mongolians wandered south and upward as far as the higher and endless Qinghai plateau of Tibet.

Indus listened to Li and his stories about Mongolia with fascination, but she had something else on her mind; what would leaving the house of Chang mean for her boy? She cared more about security for herself and little Pasang than Tibetan liberation and progress. "How can I make a living for my boy," she asks confiding over their pillow. "Start some business," Li tells her. "I will help you." Due to his position, which commanded respect from both Tibetans and Chinese civil authorities, Li soon helped her find a suitable legal location to sell food on the sidewalk. She rented a sidewalk corner in front of a store. The owner was only too happy to cooperate with the Chinese officer. Indus accepted rent money from Li as a loan, which he laughingly agreed to, already feeling a natural responsibility for Indus and little Pasang. He is often away for days on the new road project from Chengdu and is happy that Indus and little Pasang are still in the home of Chang. The ambitious noble now treats Indus as a guest. After all, he still has two women to care for him, and his little boy has his mother to care for him. In order to protect his interests with the new regime Chang has complied with new regulations and registered his now small plot and large house under his name. He registers Indus as his wife. Chinese authorities want to count and identify everyone. This facilitates control. For her part, Indus is content with life. When she looks at her boy she sees Pasang and is happy taking care of their family.

Indus gets the storeowner to let her cook in the back corner of the store. The Chinese owner is part of an emerging service economy that serves the Han immigrants. The new businessmen tend to hire their own people, while Tibetans are hired to do the harder and dirty work. Some of these help her set up a stall with a table and chairs. Hans eat on chairs, unlike Tibetans who squat down on the floor. Her little business grows, mostly due to her special sauce for the Yak meat. Indus displays new self- confidence and business sense. Tibetans who now have jobs during the day make a habit of eating at her small place.

Before long she opens a second sidewalk stall. Han customers know she is Li's woman and so they go to her stall for tea. Going to her stall is like helping another Han, even if she is Tibetan. Indus and Li are together more often now. He comes to eat at one of her stalls and visit at the small hut she now has. She still lives with Chang, but she stores supplies in her hut and has a bed made of hay to rest upon when she can. Time passes and Tibet gradually changes under Chinese control. The couple come to genuinely love each other as time passes. Each has become a natural habit for the other. And yet, Indus thinks of Pasang when Li is with her. She feels no contradiction in making love to Li. She will simply be as happy as she can be, while she waits for Pasang and watches their son grow.

Indus took so naturally to business that Li said she must be part Han. All Hans, he said, go into some form of business because they do not like to work for someone else. They like to make money on their own. At the same time that he admires her, Li is happy that Indus will not be a financial burden to him

One day a woman who came to her stall for tea tells Indus that her master Chang has died. It is Ola, one of Chang's older women. As she sipped her Chinese tea, Ola told Indus that Chang just fell down and died. Indus is shocked, for she has never suffered the death of someone close to her. She thinks about how the Chang women were now without a protector. And what will happen to little Pasang? Sensing all this, Ola pleads with Indus for help. Now that Chang's house belongs to Indus, the two older women fear that she will put them out. Indus puts the woman at ease. For now, they still have a house to live in. Meanwhile she has much to do. To please Indus as her new master, Ola offers to help find some workers who will dispose of the body out in the country for birds to take. Wealthier Tibetans were usually cremated, although wood was scarce, but now there were no wealthy Tibetans. Ola leaves the stall to return to Chang's house to give the good news to the other woman. Everything is in good hands for now. Indus sits down herself to sip some tea and reflect awhile on the new situation. She is a property owner now. Pasang and their boy have a secure future. If only Pasang would return from hiding somewhere.

Li returns after a week away on the road project that will link the north with the valley of Lhasa. The road will have to climb more than 8,000 feet over rocky mountains before it slips down to the Tibetan plateau. He tells Indus he is concerned that the road schedule is behind. Tibetans are not hard laborers since many are prisoners working off their sentence. They work at looking busy. Chinese workers from the subtropical Chengdu valley to the north do not like the high and frigid mountains of Tibet.

Li must find another labor contractor, with the death of Chang. He has come to confide in Indus like his wife. She is a good listener although she does not always understand what he is talking about. Li goes on and on as he sips down tea, which Indus is quick to pour for him. He has another responsibility now. A decision has been made in Beijing to build a full-service commercial airport near Lhasa. This will help bind the Motherland to the heart of Tibet. The nearest suitable site with enough land for a very long runway is quite far from Lhasa. An extra long runway will be necessary for landing jets, and critically necessary to allow the planes time to gain enough speed to take off in the thin air of 14,000 feet. There is much more to do, Li complains sadly. The airport will be ample and fully modern with escalators and restaurants. International service will be available soon through Beijing. Everything to Tibet must pass through Beijing.

Indus shows him through the Chang house, which he knew only in part. He is pleased with the space, and that Chang had registered the property with the new regime. This was now Indus's home with no legal problems. Li looked around the large living room with its fireplace and he felt at home. He would not have to sleep at the officers' quarters, except for appearances.

Ola, the older of Chang's women, who liked Indus from the start, told her that the two women had found another place to live. A Tibetan widower had a steady job with the government and wanted women to care for him in his small hut. Indus was happy with this arrangement. She knew that this custom was common in Tibet. It was very practical that people lived together to meet each other's needs. Matrimony as such was not important for ordinary people. Indus understood this very well because of her own personal situation.

As the two women were leaving Chang's house Ola stopped to chat with Indus. She felt more relaxed with Indus now that she was going to a new secure living arrangement of her own. She asked why Indus did not have more children. Ola was thinking of Lt. Li and how to bind him to Indus. Indus explained that she took precautions to avoid having a child with Li, although she cared for him very much. The woman reminded Indus that under Chinese control Tibetan families could have more than one child, unlike most of the rest of China. The wise old woman kept insisting that another child would bind Li to Indus. Indus explained that she was still confident Pasang would return. She wanted no children except his. Ola just shook her head and walked off. Both women had no way of knowing that except for the Han, China permitted many ethnic minorities to have more than one child. The communist party apparently did not want ethnic minorities to die off, as only one child per couple would tend to bring about. For now, Chinese planners put off the future dilemma caused by the restriction of only one child per family. Because males were favored, many couples disposed of infant girls. In time there might be a shortage of women for men to marry, as well as a shortage of labor. These global issues were beyond Indus' comprehension, she simply wanted no child except Pasang's.

After another long trip Li is anxious to see Indus and stops by one of the stalls. He surprises Indus because he wears a troubled look. He tells her quietly, as if it were a secret, that many political changes are taking place in Beijing. He will have to stay close to the office and sleep with the men to keep track of developments. He knows full well that political and personal fortunes can rise or fall overnight in the boiling pot of Beijing politics. Indus holds on to her boy especially long when he comes home from school. She had never seen Li this worried. When Li comes a few days later, again the pair sit by the fire and he starts to talk about the news coming in by radio.

The policy to break up landed estates and distribute land to individual Tibetan peasants has been very successful for more than a decade since the "peaceful liberation of Tibet" in 1950. Small landowners were selling farm products as well as cattle on the open market. They were joining a modest market economy. Li explains that rumors from Beijing talked about creating communes to replace private ownership of land. In the communes already established in other parts of China families were becoming part of a new self-governing community comprised of several families. The commune held title to all the land formerly owned by individual families.

In Tibet, like elsewhere, individual enterprise was now to be a thing of the past. All individual efforts would now be for the good of the group. Li and all the Chinese officers and troops would, of course, follow the new policy and enforce it fully. Li must give no hint of doubts about the changes for fear of losing his rank and even his life. Orders from Chairman Mao were absolute. The world's largest population was being completely reorganized. Nothing like this had ever been attempted.

By chance, Indus looked at Li's jacket thrown over a chair. It had a new emblem on the shoulders. As she picked it up for a closer look, Li called out with an authoritative tone, "You are now looking at a colonel. My commanding officer was ordered to Beijin overnight for a promotion; I hope that it's a promotion. Now I have much more to do. I will follow the ways of my former commanding officer; obey but not comply." Indus asked, " What do you mean, not comply?" Li went on to explain that ideas and rules shaped in Beijing did not always fit into conditions in the vast interior of China, like the Qinghai plateau of Tibet. As with other outlying regions of China, local officials interpreted central orders to meet local conditions.

Some flexibility was necessary to avoid an uprising like that which led to the flight of the Dalai Lama, Li said. To force compliance with anti-religious policies and lessen political support for the Dalai Lama, hundreds of monasteries had been torn down, ironically with forced monk labor. Tibetan resistance to this activity only provoked more destruction of monasteries. Now only a hundred or so monasteries remained from the several thousand before. Untold ancient records and works of art were burned at Chinese orders. Monks of all ages were forced to destroy objects sacred to them. They wondered in shock how they were going to live away from their monastery. They could no longer wear their distinctive clothes, which helped elicit alms from the faithful. Female nuns were worse off. Nuns were forced to beg for housing and food, since they had no useful skills. Li described the efforts to destroy religion, which he asserted was simply a form of poison. Indus just listened. She was learning more about the vast panorama of life. For her part, she just followed Buddhist practices without understanding them—religion was simply a custom learned from her parents. She never thought about Buddhism or cosmic ideas. Her life was defined by everyday concerns.

Sensing that Indus was interested in all this, Li went on to describe how the communist party was starting a new era in Chinese history that would outlast the various dynasties of hundreds of years before. In 1911 the last Qing dynasty ended due to public dissatisfaction with the widespread graft and corruption of the Kuomintang Party. Educated Chinese revolutionaries following western ideas, overthrew the Qing rulers and set up the Republic of China. Exotic ideas of personal freedom and republican institutions fared poorly in ordinary life. Republicanism was a thin veneer with little practical value to everyday life of peasants. The republic endured until 1949 in spite of a destructive Japanese invasion and occupation since 1937. Indeed, opposition to the Japanese occupation fed loyalty to the republic, which might have broken down earlier. Western nations in Europe and especially the United States favored the Chinese republic, but did little to help it militarily against the Japanese due to distance and insufficient commitment. The Japanese seemed embarked on a bold plan to reduce the Chinese population to make room for their own people. China had land and resources Japan needed for its plan to build an Asian empire. Western toleration for Japanese atrocities endured until their attack on Pearl Harbor in 1941. Now, helping China became part of the war against Japan.

All this information was new to Indus although much of it made little sense to her. Li was undeterred in his account of history. He had learned modern history as a requirement for officers and found it interesting, not simply a requirement. Indus was a good listener, or at least seemed to be. He was happy to tell her about how world events explained his assignment to Tibet. To gain his officer rank he had to learn much history, from the Chinese point of view, of course. His knowledge of Chinese history justified the work he was doing in Tibet. As he understood world affairs, foreign threats to China must be resisted at all costs. Controlling Tibet was of vital concern for China because of controversies with India over common borders, as well as the meddling of England while she controlled India.

Indus noticed that many more Chinese were coming to Lhasa. From Lhasa many of the newcomers went to outlying areas of Tibet where they had been assigned. Indus wondered about changes in the population. Granted that Tibetans were not limited to only one child per family like Chinese, most Tibetans could not afford to have more than one or two children. Indus wondered whether in light of free medical attention more Tibetan women would take advantage of these new services. These services in urban centers assured safe deliveries so that more infants survived, unlike children born in the hinterland. She wondered if Tibetan population could survive the immigration of Hans.

It seemed to Indus that Chinese were overwhelming the Tibet she saw around Lhasa. The number of Chinese might equal the Tibetan population before long. She just shook her head, worked hard, and looked out for her son, longing for Pasang to come back. Meanwhile, Li was good to her and she found it pleasant to make him happy. She was always thinking of Pasang as Li made love to her. She was happy enough to start singing Tibetan peasant songs to him, close to his ears. He could not understand the words- similar as they were to Han Chinese- but the music was pleasant. Indus became accustomed to Chinese customs, like bathing frequently. She acquired the use of Chinese herbs, which she rubbed over her body. This gave her a pleasant scent which pleased Li. The scents smelled so good to Li that he loved to bury his face in her armpits, which made her laugh. They were a happy couple.

Indus was curious about the growing practice of tai chi. Every day many hundreds of Chinese of all ages would gather in the huge plaza in front of the party headquarters—the largest building in downtown Lhasa. For about an hour everyone would do exercises in unison, following a leader on a tall platform. Chinese music played to keep everyone in step. Some of the Chinese music was not only new but also quite pleasant to Indus. Tibetans did not have music as part of everyday life, at least not as part of her life—and her life was typical. Nonetheless, the whole spectacle of Chinese life seemed like an invasion to her. The customs were not Tibetan, and that made them unwelcome. When she asked Li about some strange custom such as tai chi, Li said tai chi was common throughout China, so it was only natural to bring it here.

Indus was persistent as usual, so she wanted to know what tai chi was for, since so many people were involved. "You see", he went on, "in the People's Republic we find about fifty different peoples each with their own language and culture, like my own. They barely feel Chinese, and then there are the Muslims in the west that want to be free again from China. For centuries we have had to maintain control to prevent China from breaking apart. Widespread public schools for all children help build a common feeling of being Chinese. As you know, all schools are in Mandarin, even if children speak their parent's language at home. Their parents will not live forever, however. In one or two generations we will all speak one language. A scholar named Zhou Youguang, re-did ancient Chinese writing script into a modern romanized form in 1958. Zhou and a group of his students even translated the enormous Encyclopedia Britannica into modern Mandarin. These revolutionary steps have facilitated scholarship and learning wherever there is a public library. You may not know that illiteracy is being wiped out in China. Tai chi serves the purpose of promoting good health and reminding people that the Chinese life style and control are present in all parts of life." Indus remarks, "It is a gentle way to remind people of important things like that, and it looks pleasant enough. I will try it tomorrow."

"I wish more Tibetans were like you," Li continued. "As you may have heard, we have had to tear down so many monasteries because religion is poison, as Chairman Mao says. You know, oddly enough, his own mother was Buddhist. She believed that Lord Buddha appears whenever he is needed. What do you think of that? Tibetans have been poisoned by religion for many centuries. Soon after the Dalai Lama fled to India, and during the Cultural Revolution, we reduced the number of monasteries, and the monks were reduced to about 1,800. Even these are too many. Tai chi is only one way to reinforce our culture among our own and instill it among Tibetans."

Li went on, "Like our little Pasang, the vast majority of Tibetan children now attend elementary schools, little girls as well as the boys. As you know, girls got no education at all before. With technical schools here in Tibet and university openings available down in Chengdu, a new generation will be formed." Indus interjected, "Yes, at the same time, you are placing Mandarin over other languages in the movies we can see on television." Li went on, " Yes, we must educate two generations at the same time, and await a new one of children that will be free from   religious customs and rituals that are not scientific. We are no longer concerned with suppressing positive elements of Tibetan culture. Major temples like the Jokhang here in Lhasa have been spared, like the Potala Palace. Indeed, the palace has been gradually rejuvenated. Its one thousand rooms, numberless altars and some 200,000 statues have in effect been made into a museum attracting thousands of tourists annually." Indus added, "Yes, I see them come all summer long."

Li went on, "In the western region we find many thousands of Islamic people. For centuries missionaries have come there from Iran to extend their culture and religion. Some Muslims practice strange rituals. Our reports state there may be some political implications to these strange activities, although local people claim everything they do is spiritual. I may have to go there soon and tear down their main mosque in Gansu province to discourage these weird practices. We will use their own labor to make a clear impression on Muslims that we are serious. This may cause more trouble, but orders are orders."

Li acknowledged that the government faced a shortage of labor all over Tibet. Its many construction projects used up willing Tibetans, and not even the Chinese immigrants were enough of a labor pool for the work at hand. Actually, most of the Han immigrants were put to farming. They had been recruited in their native Chinese province with different customs like food and dress even though they shared the same language. The migrations of Chinese from various regions to Tibet were really an assignment that served national needs. Ethnic differences among the immigrants were of little concern on the surface, but indeed, the mix may have had the purpose of forging Chinese nationality.

Power equipment now helped plow the fields for the
communes set up during the Cultural Revolution program during
the 1960's. Quickly built homes of concrete blocks provided basic
needs for Han immigrants, and were only slightly better than
those of Tibetan farmers. The immigrants worked hard to make
conditions better, thanks to government subsidies. The immigrants
were pioneers. Their personal outlook was to improve their lot, and
in the process, change things into what they wanted. Agricultural
production increased with the use of fertilizers introduced by the
Chinese. The composition of soils and weather patterns required
study and adaptation. Although the Han were farmers mostly,
and life in the communes was tolerable, some of the males sought
permission to work in urban centers where life was more pleasant
and where they might earn some money. Some stole away from
communes without permission. Stealing away was dangerous as
officials kept track of everyone. However, a bribe usually worked to
have your work assignment and place of residence altered on the
books.

Although Li's duties were formally military, bringing
Tibet into the Chinese social system involved diverse duties. His
superiors in Beijing cared only about results, so Li had considerable
flexibility. Li's local superior found excuses to travel to Beijing
from time to time. He went to play politics in hope of gaining an
assignment out of Tibet. He hated the altitude, the cold winter, and
the Tibetans as well. As it turned out, this left Li to pretty much
control the Chinese absorption of Tibet into the Han world. As a
Mongolian, Li had come to understand and live smoothly within
the world of Hans. Hans felt superior to the other ethnic groups
in China like the Tibetans. Chairman Mao himself alluded to this
prejudice in speeches and urged Hans to stop this chauvinism
because it fed unrest at home and sparked nationalism in places
like Tibet. What was not apparent to many in China, and especially
abroad, was that the idea of China was still in process of shaping.
Holding China together was still a challenge.

The outside world did not understand the widespread

struggle to forge a feeling of nationality in China after the seizure of control by the communists in 1949. There was no overall feeling of being Chinese under Chiang Kai-shek and his wife. She was very popular in Western Europe, and especially the United States. She traveled widely seeking help for her husband as he struggled against the communists who were supported by Russia under the dictator Joseph Stalin. Communist Russia was extending its control over Eastern Europe after the Second World War ended in 1945. It sought an alliance with China, which it wanted to make into a communist ally. After the fall of the Axis Powers comprised by Germany, Italy and Japan, the so-called Cold War began. The Soviet Union sought global domination starting with Western Europe. Within a year after the fall of Hitler's Germany in 1945, former allies were now mortal enemies due to the Soviet Union's plans for global domination. Since the United States and the Soviet Union each had missiles and nuclear weapons that could wipe out all life in the other, the Cold War took on nonviolent methods to decide global domination. Far away Tibet was one piece in the global game for power. China therefore believed it was essential that it control its territory more tightly. That meant Tibet must be absorbed.

President Eisenhower led the European powers against the Soviet Union's actions to dominate Eastern Europe. This leadership was necessary because the victorious French and English allies were devastated by the costs of their victory over Germany. President Roosevelt had died before the German surrender, and his Vice President, Harry Truman, took office. Under Truman, the United States, largely by itself, defeated Japan that same year, by frightening it into surrender by dropping atomic bombs on two major Japanese cities. Truman's successor, President Eisenhower, went to the extent of befriending the Communist Marshal Tito because Tito insisted on keeping Yugoslavia free of Soviet control, even if it meant war. Russia under Stalin wisely left communist Yugoslavia alone under American protection. Likewise, to hinder and undermine newly-formed Communist China, Eisenhower sent the mighty Seventh Fleet to help the island of Taiwan remain free from China. He also sent CIA agents to Nepal to train Tibetan refugees how to cause problems for China by organizing resistance to its new rule there. Pasang's flight to Nepal and his experiences there was a very small episode of this vast international drama.

Tibetans knew nothing about how they figured into the Cold War. Control of Tibet was vital to China in its historical contest with India for control of the Himalayan plateau. While England had ruled in India for two centuries it supported Indian claims to Tibet, sending agents to Lhasa with old-fashioned weapons for the Tibetan army. As a spiritual leader, the young Dalai Lama was not a military general, thus Tibetans could offer only slight resistance to the Chinese troops. The Chinese moved in peacefully for the most part, and on foot. At the start, Chinese control in Tibet was almost gentle because it neutralized the upper class Tibetans with bribes and used modest force only when necessary. Most Tibetan troops put up little resistance to the Chinese as they saw upper class Tibetans lose power. Tibetan troops witnessed with glee land of the hated nobility distributed to peasants like themselves. Tibetan noble families had over time gathered control of the lowlands and the richer soil. To partition this choice land to peasants was revolutionary in several respects. The source of wealth for the nobility was taken away and with it, social power. Peasants were now landowners with the potential for a better life in most respects.

The Dalai Lama, for his part, spoke out against violent resistance, hoping the Chinese would keep their promises to respect Tibet customs and religion. The announced intentions of the Chinese sounded friendly. The Dalai Lama sent word out to even nomad Tibetans in the west to avoid violence. Word from the Dalai Lama was like word from god. To all appearances, the Dalai Lama was accepting the non-religious changes introduced by the Chinese.

In Lhasa Li ordered the formation of neighborhood committees elected by residents of each district. For three-year terms the chairman of each neighborhood committee was a Chinese Communist Party appointee, however. The Chinese were in firm control of the new democratic processes. And yet, democratization became widespread in Tibetan life, although political power was limited. Before the Chinese occupation, Tibetan women were excluded from any public affairs. Under Chinese control they could now vote and gain positions as diverse as local police and judgeships. They could even gain election to the new Tibetan People's Congress. The neighborhood committees served as a mechanism to involve Tibetans in self-government, and also to maintain order. The committees also served the vital function of maintaining identification of residents. Indus declined an offer to join the committee of her district. Everyone knew she was Li's woman and expected her to take a public role, but she was too busy with her new business. Li did not press her on civic involvement because he was content that she was home whenever he came and wanted her company. Indus understood this, for she had studied her man well. She knew how much freedom she had to bend regulations that applied to others.

Li was called away for several weeks because highwaymen were active again. Greater movement of people was possible due to new roads. This made robberies along the roads more common. Because Tibetans were almost all Buddhists, physical harm was rare during the robberies. Getting robbed on the road seemed almost part of everyday life. No one was hurt and victims had little to give up to begin with. Robbers were amateurs, commonly. They had left their plot of land and took leave from their family due to hardship. Robbing caravans or lonely travelers was a part-time occupation.

In some cases families walked for many miles to favorite religious sites to worship. These treks went on for weeks sometimes, going from one holy site to another. The worshipers commonly prostrated themselves face down on the road and prayed, then got up and took a few steps only to prostrate themselves again. Other travelers simply walked by these pilgrims respectfully. Bandits rarely bothered pilgrims and robbed only the better prospects. Robbers were not easy for police to find, for victims were reluctant to cooperate with the police, which were usually Chinese. The new regime sought to eliminate this traditional Tibetan activity because it discouraged growing trade.

Although the Chinese disrupted traditional Tibetan culture, some new elements were gradually forming. The new egalitarian composition of Tibetan society saw the formation among Tibetans of a new independent outlook and greater personal initiative. The elimination of nobility and land distribution had a gradual beneficial effect. Granted the Tibet Autonomous Region was dominated by the Chinese, Tibetan individuals could aspire to prosper as long as they did not contest Chinese domination of the TAR (Tibet Autonomous Republic). Although the TAR was nominally in charge of all domestic affairs within Tibet, all foreign affairs, currency, and the military were in central Chinese hands. Even then, a new Tibetan society was emerging, and the old ways would survive only on part.

Despite the many changes in all walks of life, religious traditions survived. Tibetans counted the days until the next Buddhist festival. Some festivals went on for several days with thousands gathering for the religious activities and socializing. Beautiful and intricate costumes and music amazed country folk. Except when they were brought out for festivals, the beautiful outfits were carefully stored in the monasteries. Many outfits were centuries old. The restricted use of these beautiful costumes explained their survival.

In some festivals horse racing attracted extra large crowds due to the excitement. Among Tibetans horse racing had a religious function. Mongolians, as well as the Chinese army, sought Tibetan horses over the centuries. Thousands of Tibetan horses were sold annually. Due to the high altitude where they bred freely on the Tibetan plateau, their larger lungs gave them stamina that armies sought for their cavalry. Tibetan horses were smaller than others, but they were tougher than lowlander steeds.

While Li was away on assignment again, Indus could leave her teashop in good hands while she moved about. She saw some elements of Tibetan society for the first time. She was becoming Tibetan in a broader sense. Resentment to the growing number of Chinese created a sense of nationalism she never felt before. Her visit to the Summer Palace of the Dalai Lama was an eye opener. The secluded palace was now a museum open to the public. During good weather its vast gardens were filled with families enjoying food spread out on blankets. Musicians walked about accepting pay to entertain. In one area plays were offered on a new stage. These plays depicted Tibetan culture and history. Since about half of Tibetans lived in and around Lhasa, all this activity was reinforcing what it was to be Tibetan. Indeed this new regime was facilitating the exposure of more Tibetans to their cultural heritage for the first time.

All the time, however, more Han Chinese were assigned to Tibet to set up all manner of modern institutions, forms of production and services. The regime set up a large television production and broadcasting center. It was one of the largest new buildings in Lhasa. At first the only television sets were visible in shopping center windows for passersby to see. Gradually even modest hotels provided TV in lobbies. The programs were all in Chinese, but were very diverse in subject matter. Programming included what the government thought was newsworthy around the world, political indoctrination, education and entertainment. As more urban Tibetans acquired TV sets at home, the world was opening up before them through Chinese eyes. Curiously, viewers could see TV commercials for American motor oils in Mandarin.

Indus' young boy was growing taller than most Tibetans and he was completely bilingual. Indus called him Pasang like his father. The pair spoke Tibetan at home, but school life was solely in Mandarin. As Indus passed a school during one of her walks, she remembered that Li had taken pride in Pasang's progress in school. Over time they had become like a family. Soon he might qualify for studies away from home in Chengdu, which was far down from the Tibetan plateau. To get to Chengdu one must go over the Zar Gama Pass at some 15,000 feet. A new road would allow travel by trucks and automobiles for the first time. Travel was slow due to the difficulties of the terrain. Li was responsible for advancing this vital project.

Not far above sea level, this large and prosperous provincial capital had special schools for youths from diverse ethnic minorities. In these schools a new generation of youth was taking shape. As students from many ethnic backgrounds specialized in practical fields like education, farming, mechanics, engineering and medicine, they were also becoming Chinese communists in mind and body. Since classes were integrated, the young boys and girls from many regions also had new experiences, unlike their largely segregated life back home.

As usual Indus was asking Li questions about China, and particularly its intent of absorbing Tibet. She could not understand what value Tibet had for China. The land was poor except in some fertile places belonging to nobles, so that terraces crawled up the mountain slopes for meager crop yields. Without answering Indus on that score, Li said he felt at home because for centuries Mongolians had migrated to Tibet to survive. Moving in all directions, except to the arctic north, thousands of Mongolians migrated south up to the plateau of Tibet on horseback. Most Mongolians settled peacefully, but others were so violent that over time "Mongolian" became synonymous with warriors.

During one intimate conversation, Li whispered that his father took in a pretty Mongolian girl. She felt lucky to cook and keep the soldier warm at night. The girl was smart enough to remember where her interest lay so she made her man happy. The soldier's rank rose as time went by and the girl's belly finally swelled. As an infant Li learned Mandarin from his father and Mongolian from his mother. Indus laughed at Li's exaggeration that Mongolian boys like him learned to ride as soon as they learned to walk.

When Li's father was to be transferred back to central China,

he took Li's mother aside and said, " Look, our son will have to
be more Han than a Han. He will face discrimination unless he
moves among us and acts like a Han. " The boy's height gave him
an appearance of more years than he had. This made it easier for
his father to enlist him into an army training reserve unit. His
father's rank helped overcome the obstacle of the boy's youth.
Young Li never forgot his father's stern admonition as his departure
approached. Face to face, and looking deep into his eyes, his father
said sternly that in the army he must always be better than everyone
else of his rank. After a long pause, Li breathed in a low and sad
voice that he never saw his father again.

As years went by young Li kept being better in all assignments
than his fellows, so promotions came one after the other. His
ambitious nature responded to the announcement for volunteers
to be part of the liberation of Tibet. From what he knew from army
sources, Chairman Mao and the army had chased President Chiang
Kai-shek out of China to his refuge on the island of Taiwan. The
new Chinese forces now wanted to re-incorporate Tibet into the
new People's Republic of China. As a half Mongolian, Li felt a bond
with Tibet. He knew that many of his people had gone to live up
there over the centuries, and he saw a professional opportunity on
that high plateau.

The young Dalai Lama was just fourteen years old in 1950.
Surely his advisors would see the benefits of becoming a part of
China formally. The British in India for over a century tried to
influence one Dalai Lama after another, and India maintained
that practice after gaining its independence from England.
Indeed several border wars along crucial mountain passes kept
up hostilities between India and China high up in the Himalayas.
The Nationalist government of China under Chiang Kai-shek
claimed Tibet since the founding of the Republic of China in
1911, but could never establish effective rule over it. For its part,
Imperial Russia claimed parts of Tibet, but these claims were
largely dormant since the Russian Revolution of 1910. Although the
crumbling Russian Empire occupied the communist revolutionaries

for decades at home, Chinese leaders never forgot Russian claims to parts of Tibet.

The rest of the world knew only that Tibet was a distant and exotic place holding the highest mountains in the world, and an exotic Buddhist religion. The government of Adolf Hitler had high-level proponents asserting that traces of the legendary Aryan race might be found in Tibet. It sent a secret expedition there in the latter 1930's that returned in frustration.

The United Nations, formed after the end of World War II in 1945, showed no interest in getting involved in Tibetan matters as China voiced intentions to absorb Tibet. China was granted permanent membership in the UN Security Council to establish a realistic balance of power globally. This gave it power to veto any serious action by the Security Council regarding Tibet.

Communist North Korea invaded democratic South Korea in 1950 as part of the communist thrust for global power. Communist China took the side of North Korea in order to have a stake in the future of that neighbor. South Korea was nearly overrun until the Security Council surprisingly organized an alliance to save South Korean independence. Under American leadership an international coalition of countries confronted North Korean troops.

The United States was now involved in another war in Asia; first Japan and now Korea. The United States and volunteer nations gathered by the United Nations saved South Korea, in spite of several hundred thousand Chinese "volunteers" that fought alongside North Koreans against the UN troops, comprised by mostly Americans. A truce, which brought stalemated hostilities to an end, is still in effect today, without a formal peace treaty. Young Lieutenant Li was aware of all this political history because he made it his business to study and exceed his fellow officers in every way, as his father had demanded. He never let his superiors know just how much he knew; this was bad politics and fostered jealously. Indus was a good listener and so he vented his feelings about politics and concerns to her because now she could follow the events. She often asked penetrating questions, much to his delight.

Indus in time had two teahouses catering mostly to Chinese. There she overheard political discussions because she had learned Mandarin and this was most useful. One of the teahouses had grown into a restaurant. Her enterprise stemmed from the economic policy of China in the early stages of its occupation. The plan was to liberate Tibetans from feudalism and make the semi-autonomous region free to prosper and progress into the modern world. A small Tibetan middle class was slowly emerging. At the same time the Chinese immigrants were prospering due to their industrious nature and government subsidies. Chinese officers and Tibetans who were better off became steady customers for Indus. She had a gracious way with important Chinese who knew who she was.

She could barely serve the seventy-five or so dishes that even a modest three star Chinese restaurant must have, not to mention the many more entrees of a four star restaurant. This would be close to impossible. She managed to steer a middle course to satisfy Chinese officers and business people who were sophisticated about their food. These demanded quality, which she provided thanks to good Chinese cooks. Ever inquisitive, Indus sought lessons on Chinese dishes, and watched her cooks closely. She learned that Chinese food was a vast world of tastes and flavors unlike simple Tibetan dishes. She learned that regions of China had their own vast array of dishes. She proudly displayed the three stars over the name of her restaurant. It was unthinkable not to be able to meet the standard claimed by three stars. The landlord from whom she rented space charged a modest fee because he knew about her relationship with Col. Li, and where his interest lay. Everything was possible with the support of her Colonel Li. Thus in time Indus was able to buy the restaurant site. She was part of the new Chinese economic establishment.

In the course of a discussion over dinner, Li told her about fewer problems with Tibetan militants, and how reports from Beijing hinted at relaxation of border controls at the Indian and Nepalese borders. Indus had no idea where Pasang was hiding as she heard this. She only heard rumors that Tibetans were in India and Nepal, thanks to some who returned from trading there. Her hopes sprang up like a warm fire at this news, but she kept all this to herself. Not a word of this passed to even young Pasang, who was now a young man. He had been an infant when Chang died. Indus had told him that Chang was his father to protect him from association with his real father. Indus had imagined for years that Pasang was on a list of Tibetans wanted by the Chinese. Now she imagined with suppressed excitement that Pasang might be able to come back and be together with both of them.

CHAPTER FOUR
Study In Chengdu

Young Pasang was now down in southern China studying animal husbandry in Chengdu. Col. Li had arranged for his attendance at this special school although he was not quite old enough. He gave Pasang the same firm advice he got from his father in Mongolia, but in a friendlier manner. He had grown to care for Pasang like a son and wanted the best for him. Pasang returned the warm sentiments and paid heed to everything Li had said to him during his youth.

Many hundreds of Tibetan boys and girls were attending schools down in semi-tropical China. In return for their educational benefits they promised to return to Tibet as professionals. They would be a new generation of leaders in diverse fields to gradually modernize life in Tibet. They would have to compete, however, with the steady migration of Han Chinese brought in by the central government, but their employment was assured. The official government policy intended to alter the population of that vast plateau, making it primarily Chinese over time. In spite of professional education for some Tibetans, it seemed that Tibetans would become a minority in their own land. This intent was clear to observant Tibetans.

Young Pasang was one of the many officially recognized ethnic groups selected to study in Chengdu. The students all had a native form of Chinese, although all of them had been perfecting their Mandarin since public school. This was the only language in which they could communicate with other students. The school was a United Nations in session, without translators. Pasang was old enough to look at girls with lust, and often did. He enjoyed the variety among the students. They came from all over China. One girl was already looking at him when he noticed her the first time. The school frowned upon social or personal relations outside of studies, but given human nature couples discreetly sought out companionship when possible. Intense studies made this difficult, but not impossible for young people who were curious about students from other provinces.

Young Pasang studied hard in Chengdu and imagined working at animal husbandry alongside his mother. The looks of his fellow students varied widely, and among their own, they spoke in their native tongue. The languages were similar to Mandarin, but different enough so that they could not understand others well. Included among the studies, nationalistic and communist ideology featured prominently. Nation building was as important to the government as the specialties the students would take to their provinces after two years. Pasang saw the connection between the Chinese programs in Tibet and what he imagined was happening elsewhere in The People's Republic. He had no idea of the size of China, but he imagined it must be vast in view of all the different young people and the bragging they did about their home province. All the maps on the walls placed China in the center, with the rest of the world on the fringes.

One particular girl always seemed to be looking at him when he happened to see her. She too was studying animal husbandry to take back to Jilin Province. When they sat together at a meal, not really by chance, Ming told him about Jilin. Endless fertile fields surrounded her home. Plentiful grass fed cattle and horses. She told him about how more food production was becoming a priority in view of increasing population. The traditional life of horsemen and families wandering far across the steppes must give way to settled and organized life. Such changes brought her to study in Chengdu. Pasang could listen to Ming go on and on because her native, musical speaking affected her Mandarin. And besides, she was pretty and always cheerful.

Her home near Harbin was farther north than Korea, she pointed out. Koreans and some Chinese claimed that a huge local mountain was sacred and the source of their strength and future greatness. She could not believe Pasang's stories about how high the Himalayas were. There was plenty of time for them to compare stories about how great their own province was. They were constantly among the stock and learning about their care and breeding. On one occasion they led in a cow to a stall for breeding. They watched with fascination as the bull mounted the cow as the cow grunted. Ming took out the cow, smiling at Pasang after the encounter. Her smile prompted no special thought at the time. She was always smiling. But this time her smile was special in a way he would soon see.

At the end of the day as he was washing his face in the co-ed bathroom, Ming came in from behind. She wrapped her arms around him tightly, catching him by surprise. As he tried to dry his face he felt her right hand reach down into his trousers. Startled, he tried to pull away but she held him tightly. Her right hand slipped down to where she took hold of his organ which promptly rose up. Surprised by the new sensation he looked into the mirror and saw Ming's face looking over his shoulder with a big grin. They heard students come into the washroom so Ming backed away. In the two seconds of looking into each other's eyes, an understanding was sealed.

That evening after supper they met in one of the barns. In a stall covered with fresh hay they began to enjoy each other. This was Pasang's first love and he didn't know much about what to do, beyond the basics like the stock they had watched. But Ming knew about little things to do, and he was a rapid learner. As they lay there a while in luxury they could hear whispering in another stall; they were not alone. Pregnancy was no problem because the college clinic could take care of that inconvenience. Lovemaking became a happy routine and their fellow students knew they were a couple.

As Pasang came to know some of the instructors well enough, he came to learn how little regard the local people had for officials in Beijing. These were almost foreigners to the people of Sichuan, and the officials from the north returned the sentiments. Sichuan was a fertile region with a rich cultural heritage. This region was largely independent from Beijing during the Republican era under Chiang Kai-shek. Not even the brutal Japanese occupation along the coast and northern settlements in Manchuria had affected Sichuan much. The communist regime after 1949, however, did want to control the region and make it an integral part of the People's Republic. Commonplace tai chi exercises in the central parks were only one of many ways the populace was being trained to be Chinese. Several thousand people of all ages in parks doing exercises in unison to martial music all over the country testified to central party control.

Pasang and Ming had occasion to walk around the lovely city of Chengdu. The wide avenues and parks were impressive to the pair. The surroundings were so different from their own back home, especially the heavy traffic and countless stores. Ming did know about Changchun, capital of Jilin Province and the center of movie production in China. It was a smaller provincial city of about ten million people. Pasang noted with humor that its population rivaled Tibet's. The vast lots of movie sets were more extensive than you could walk around in one day, and closely guarded. Ming explained she was addicted to movies and had visited the studios ounce, allowed admittance thanks to the influence of a family friend. She saw the numerous sets for the movie on the last emperor of China. She could not forget their beauty, and learned the sets would be used for other movies later.

The municipal museum fascinated the couple and both found themselves admiring ancient Chinese culture dating back before western civilization. The full meaning behind the paintings and objects of so long ago did not really sink in, however. Pasang and Ming were connected to this tradition, but it was not really their own. The Yuan, Ming and Qing dynasties stretched back many centuries up to the rise of the Chinese Republic in 1912, but these were only names. The displays of intricate art made an impression on the two as they had never seen such delicate art at home.

Sichuan had a life of its own since anyone could remember. It was not like the rest of China, and it took pride in ignoring dictates from Beijin. In spite of the one child per family rule, and fines for a second child, it was not uncommon to see larger families in Sichuan. Indeed, the great reformers like Deng Xiaoping and Premier Zhao Ziyang were from Sichuan. After the death of Chairman Mao they led China into a new contemporary era. Publicly everyone lamented the loss of their great leader, like a matter of religious faith, but in the close circle of friends they were relieved. Many officials worked to unravel Mao's lifetime of work. Mao's widow and her circle of political friends had been infamous for favoritism and interfering with Mao's programs for their personal benefit. Out of respect for Mao, his widow was forced into retirement, but some of her associates did not fare as well. They were quickly executed, leaving her stranded and out of grace.

While maintaining the one child policy as a matter of national survival, many new policies were quickly put into effect. Deng went so far as to say that, "Its all right to make money." He also stated that progress in the west was connected to the ethics of Christianity. Such talk was no less than amazing to traditionalists. Communes throughout China were soon replaced by private ownership. Many communes became businesses and prospered after new taxes. Linked by better communication the profound changes took hold everywhere including Tibet. The largest communist society was on the way to becoming the largest capitalist society.

Before long both Pasang and Ming prepared to leave their school and Chengdu. They would return to their own distinctive lands, traveling in opposite directions. Pasang realized all these new experiences would soon be memories, including his charming Ming. His mother was always on his mind, thanks to her letters. In his letters home he never mentioned Ming, as much as he had come to care for her. She was not Tibetan, after all.

It seemed like only yesterday when he took the long bus ride from Lhasa down the tortuous new road to Chengdu. Now he was finished and saying farewell to his friends at school. They too would be scattering back to their homes all over the interior of China, enjoying the status of graduates from the Nationalities Institute in Chengdu. During their last night in the barn Pasang and Ming knew they would never be together again, but they did not speak of it as they enjoyed each other for the last time.

CHAPTER FIVE
A New Tibet

The next day Pasang thought of Ming as the bus struggled up the winding road towards the plateau of Tibet. The road was now paved and smooth, not like two years before. In some locations one could look across a valley and see the excavations for the railroad, crawling its way up from Chengdu. He thought about wonderful Ming going in the opposite direction to the vast plains in the north. He was going home to the high and mountainous south.

Sitting next to him was a distinguished looking older man. They leaned into each other on turns and this led to their conversation. The man noticed that Pasang had a shirt with the logo of his institute, and he asked about it. Pasang told the man about his studies and plans for helping Tibet improve animal husbandry. He pointed to some wild horses along the road and how these were becoming scarcer and less hardy because of uncontrolled inbreeding. The seats in front of them were facing back towards them. One of two young girls facing them had her eyes fixed on Pasang. He gave this little notice at the time and went on with his dialogue with the stranger.

The man was on his way to Lhasa as one of the founding professors for an autonomous university in Tibet. The Tibet

Autonomous Region (TAR), as the government was called, sought its own learning center but had no professors. The founding staff had to be Chinese since Tibet had no educational social group of teachers. The gentleman said that in time the university would undertake preserving Tibetan culture and the publication of books on Tibetan history, folklore and religion. Some units related to the university would do research and publish materials on soils, fertilizers, and crops. The professor pointed out that the idea was to make Tibet self-sufficient and healthier, rather than a dependency on the Motherland. Pasang nodded in agreement. The young girl was still looking at Pasang, but she was also fascinated by the older man's conversation.

Pasang had learned in school that over the centuries India, China and even England had wanted to control this faraway plateau with its vast barren steppes, and countless monasteries. Why did China want Tibet, Pasang asked in a burst of frankness? The two were now talking with a frankness born of isolation from their usual social setting. Their regular associates would never know what they said to each other.

"Our Motherland is very ancient," the old man went on. "Ever since the leaders among early warriors came to call themselves emperors, they sought to expand in all directions and control all they could grab as personal property. The endless Mongolian plains made them want to keep getting more land and subjects. They passed on their power to their sons, thus beginning a long string of family dynasties. Genghis Khan was the founder of the first Mongol Empire that came to dominate most of central China. His son, Kublai Khan, was the first emperor that came to be known by westerners.

Kublai Khan's ambitions knew no bounds. After conquering northern China and absorbing the Koreans, who still dislike us Chinese, he organized a naval fleet that grew to 4,400 vessels of all sizes to invade Japan. In keeping with his policy, Japan was offered peace to become a vassal to Kublai Khan. Japan refused the honor. The invasion of Japan ended in disaster when a storm, larger than anyone had seen before, struck the fleet. The storm drowned most of the Mongols, Chinese, and Korean troops that had been conscripted for the invasion. Japan has remained free from China ever since." Pasang interjected, " Did not Japan return the favor with its invasion of China about fifty years ago?" "Yes," the professor said, "That invasion failed also. People should stay in their own land." Out of courtesy, Pasang did not bring up why China was in Tibet.

"Much depends on what you have in mind, however." The professor went on, " The rulers of the Ming dynasty set out to make their empire extend far beyond the land mass of China during the so-called Middle Ages in Europe. Can you imagine? A fleet of 62 large ships about 400 feet long with soldiers, physicians, astrologers, and craftsmen set out along the coast towards India. It was a long and hazardous journey. Their mission was to spread Chinese culture through trade and friendly relations. Chinese influence in every respect would result from the new relations. Everywhere they stopped along the shores they served as ambassadors for China. Over several years and seven voyages, some of the fleet went as far as Africa, bringing home a giraffe for the emperor. Some of the Chinese adventurers traveled by land as far as Mecca and returned to the fleet before it left for home. Before long several states in the Middle East sent ambassadors to Beijing, establishing religious and trading relations between Western Europe and Asia long before the Portuguese or Spaniards.

Zheng He, the admiral of these ventures, and a favorite of the emperor, fell out of favor with his successor. It may have been jealousy. The new Emperor Yung Lu, in a major historical shift for China, decided to isolate his empire from the rest of the world. He ordered that the entire fleet be burned, and that sailing by his subjects be restricted to the coastline. Zheng He lived out his life in the shadows. Foreigners were no longer welcome, even if some of his lieutenants had extended Chinese influence as far as Iran. What an idiot, that Yung Lu!" the old man muttered.

"The Spanish and Portuguese explorers, after Columbus made his amazing voyages, tried to establish relations with China with mixed success because foreigners were still not welcome in China. During the 1800's England, France and the Dutch established trading posts along the coast of China, but these were backed by military power. China resisted opening up to the world even for trade. After centuries of isolation the last Qing dynasty became so weakened by corruption and disunity that the central government was falling apart. That's when some western-oriented reformers overthrew the rotting regime and established the Republic of China in 1912. China opened its doors to the rest of the world once again."

The professor went on, " I am sure your have learned about the Japanese invasion of China during the 1930's, and its expulsion by allied Western powers in 1945. Soon after this, our Chairman, Mao Zedong, and communist patriots began the struggle to found the People's Republic of China. Now we are growing to be a major world power. We don't have to invent most of what we need, we simply copy what Japan and Western economies have invented until we can improve it. What is happening in Tibet is part of the overall plan." The professor seemed tired and stopped for a minute, and then said, " I apologize for the lecture on history. I could not stop once I started." All this fascinated the girls and Pasang. The professor had spoken with such passion. Pasang saw more clearly now how Tibet fit into the historical Chinese mentality to expand in all directions.

In response to a polite question from the professor, it turned out the two girls were nurses. They too had received their training in Chengdu. The girl Pasang noticed looking at him was the most talkative. Her name was Chu and she described how important it was to vaccinate children, since about one in four Tibetan infants died in their first year. The second girl laughed out loud that her friend Chu preferred to vaccinate men in their butt rather than the shoulder. As Pasang heard Chu go on about the work she was looking forward to, he noticed for the first time that she was rather pretty. She looked somewhat like Ming who must be back to Changchun by now, since there was a fast train to that northern province. The bus from Chengdu to Lhasa was under way slowly because of the challenge posed by the terrain.

The passengers fell asleep as the bus went over the mountain pass and dropped down into the valley the next morning. From two thousand feet elevation in Chengdu they were now at 14,000 feet, in Lhasa . This two-day trip would have taken several weeks on foot before. The young people took the ease of travel for granted as the bus pulled into the depot in Lhasa. Most of the milling passengers in the crowded depot had on the customary white scarfs for travelers. Pasang noted that among the travelers many were Chinese soldiers including young women proudly dressed in their smart uniforms. Chu boldly asked Pasang if he lived in Lhasa like she did. The professor said he was going to look for a restaurant called The Green Lotus that was recommended to him in Chengdu. " I will ask around for it. Maybe the tourist office will know." Pasang smiled at hearing that his mother's restaurant was known beyond Lhasa and he offered to show the professor where to find it. The four travelers bid farewell. Chu went her way, but not before she waited for the two men to reach the restaurant. She took note where she might find Pasang later. He casually waved goodbye to the nurses as they went their way, but he could not imagine that he was a marked man by one of them.

At The Green Lotus Pasang introduced the professor to Indus who was delighted to see her son again. He looked taller and needed a shave. The professor stayed on at the restaurant to sample the famous food. Pasang was more self-confident now and talked on and on about his studies as he and his mother walked home. Indus chuckled about how he would soon help her with the growing number of pigs she was raising for the restaurant. The Han preferred pork to beef, she said. The restaurant was in good hands so the pair talked well into the evening until Indus went back to collect the day's returns.

Pasang noticed that Colonel Li did not come home that

evening. He was long since accustomed to Li's relationship with his mother. That was how things were for a long time, and besides, he liked Li. Indus said he was called away to Beijing and had been gone for two weeks. Television news hinted at numerous changes in governmental posts since the passing away of Chairman Mao. Li had told her that military changes were also taking place, but he knew little about this so far. Some high officials had been transferred to western posts, which amounted to punishment or lack of confidence. He was not worried personally, he had told her, but he did wonder why he was called back to Beijing.

The answer became clear a week later. Li came by one afternoon, which was not the usual time. He said he had been back in Lhasa for several days tied down at the office. He was wearing the uniform of a Lieutenant General. His superior had been transferred overnight, and Li was now Commanding Officer of Chinese forces in Tibet. He would work closely with the Tibet Autonomous Region government in civic affairs, but he would handle all military matters in the TAR. Alongside the Communist Party officials in Lhasa, Lt. General Li was at the top of the pyramid. As usual he did not talk much about politics because he needed rest at home with Indus. He did congratulate Pasang on his graduation and said he wanted him to accompany some Chinese specialists who were inspecting herding areas. Pasang was delighted to have his first official function and outlet for his new training.

For meals Pasang went to The Green Lotus to eat because he had come to prefer Chinese cuisine, which he found enormously more varied and better tasting than Tibetan food. At the restaurant one evening the professor appeared and the two sat down to talk over a meal. The old man looked younger and soon explained why. The challenge of founding a small university alongside the newly imported Chinese professors was invigorating. Some Tibetan scholars had been identified, thanks to TV announcements. They were delighted by the prospects of gathering important Tibetan religious scrolls and historical documents for publication in modern script. Items that had for centuries been kept in seclusion for the use of priests and monks would now be available to the public. A new Tibet Nationalities Institute was in formation as a branch of the Central Institute for Nationalities in Beijing. A nationwide effort was underway to preserve the culture of ethnic minorities. Rather than smother ethnic cultures, China after Mao saw them as a source of strength as long as national identity was paramount. To help assure national identity, all public instruction was in Mandarin. Sources of information from all over the world were being translated into Mandarin, including the Encyclopedia Britannica. The professor chuckled that the encyclopedia was already about ten years out of date in scientific matters by the time it appeared because it took that long to compose and print the many volumes. Even then, except for science, it was a valuable source of information that was now available in all the country's universities. As for Tibet, the professor noted, public access to ancient cultural content and artifacts would only strengthen the region and China as well.

During their long supper lovely Chu walked in dressed in her nurse uniform. She did not let on that she had come in several times in hope of seeing Pasang. She feigned surprise at the meeting and joined the two at their invitation. Pasang asked the professor what he saw for Tibet's future in light of his many years. The professor paused and then said, "Our peoples go back farther than the Egyptians and Greeks. One dynasty after the other followed for centuries. These families of warriors were often like the gangsters of American movies. They ruled with brutal power. Their major value lay in the stability they offered in their expanding domains. These domains reached as far as Iran and Eastern Europe for a while. Granted some emperors were humane and wise, but most simply enjoyed their power and spent much time making babies. Their boys went into the military and the daughters were given as presents to loyalists or brides for political alliances."

Chu laughed at this, and Pasang liked her laughter. She had a way of raising her head and closing her eyes for a moment. The professor went on, "When the Qing Dynasty dissolved in

1911 China had a brief and futile experience with republicanism until Marxism took over under our Chairman Mao and the Communist Party in 1949. Since Chairman Mao died we have been modernizing and opening up to the world. We are still ruled by one party and there is no way to change that, but perhaps with enough economic growth we can find our way to a better life." The professor was always detailed with his remarks to questions put by Pasang. The professor was always a professor.

Indus walked about the restaurant attending to the customers. She noticed that the young nurse was very casual with the two men. The nurse was not a typical Tibetan girl who would be withdrawn in such company. Indeed, a Tibetan girl would not be in such a setting. Pasang was obviously enjoying her company. This made Indus curious, so she sat down with the group to see this girl up close. The three went on with their conversation while Indus just sipped her tea and discreetly looked at Chu up and down, listening to her conversation intently.

CHAPTER SIX

BACK IN NEPAL

Tibetans refugees and merchants coming to Nepal kept Pasang aware of events back home. He could always spot Tibetans because most touched foreheads or stuck out their tongues upon greeting. Nepalese did not do that. The refugees told him about the great numbers of geese, cranes and golden eagles that flew back and forth over the high passes, and political events as well. At home Tibetan nomads, like everyone else in Tibet, were being pressured into communes and some preferred to leave Tibet rather than live in one location under the control of a social unit. These left behind family members cared for by others in the communes. Surviving in Nepal was not easy because Nepalese resented their growing numbers. Refugees trapped rabbits and other game, sleeping out where they could find a spot. The lucky ones found low paying work in the emerging tourist industry.

Since the early 1950's Nepal had opened up to tourists after centuries of discouraging visitors. The successful conquest of Mount Everest in 1953 had made Nepal a tourist attraction. Hundreds of tourists before, turned into a stream of thousands annually. Hotels now numbered over twenty, hiring many workers and forming a service economy. A new national park surrounded Mt. Everest, which was called Goddess of the Universe by Nepalese.

Sagarmatha Park was an idea of the Harvard- educated, young king of Nepal.

Urgent measures were needed to preserve the environment of the region, especially the disappearing forests and shrubs used for building and fires. It was a novel idea of the king to stop the ruthless deforestation in spite of public resistance. Increased tourism was affecting many parts of Nepalese life. Several thousand Sherpa guides lived in the vast park to assist mountain climbers. The Sherpa became a kind of folk hero after the conquest of Mt. Everest, calling themselves "Tigers of the Snow," a name which others took up to call them. The income from tourists was changing the economy and opening new opportunities. The Tibetan workers were the lowest paid workers, but they took any work they could find, gradually finding a way to survive in their country of refuge. Pasang always sought out Tibetans for news about home.

The king was undertaking the modernization of Nepal. He did not imagine making his country into a New England setting that he knew, but he saw how modern elements introduced from abroad could help make a far a better life in Nepal, while preserving traditional customs. Thus a new elected parliament shared political decision-making with the king. Gradually the new institution took hold, and Nepalese came to appreciate that their king willingly gave up some of his powers. Tara's husband had been part of this historic transition.

Maoist sympathizers inspired by China were agitating for revolution, and so the king was moving ahead of their demands to avoid making the Maoists into martyrs for reforms. The Maoists were particularly critical of the Peace Corps workers scattered around Nepal working in schools and clinics. Their projects lessened the need for Maoist reforms, and were introducing a positive and self-help approach to peasant life. The king clearly had a good plan in place. The newly installed President of Nepal joined the effort to promote Nepal by luring thousands of tourists and pilgrims to visit the area. Nepal now more openly identified itself as the birthplace of Buddha 2,555 years ago.

New Zealanders adopted Nepal after the newly-decorated Sir Edmund Hillary mounted the peak named after Sir George Everest. Everest had surveyed the site in 1865 and was the first to call it the highest point on the planet. While the Nepalese called the mountain Sagarmatha, the world came to call it Mount Everest. New Zealanders came to feel like they were part of the mountain because one of their own had reached the top first. Nepalese were proud because the climb was made from the Nepalese side and a local Sherpa had helped Hillary get to the top.

Tara explained to Pasang how Hillary's love for Nepal grew steadily. In gratitude for the help by Sherpas and the charms of the isolated society, he undertook to raise money in New Zealand to build schools for Sherpa children. All this good will only made things worse in some unexpected ways, Tara pointed out. More New Zealanders now came to see Nepal and help out like Hillary. Stories about the climb increased and were elaborated, especially in view of the fact that news of the successful climb reached England at the very time of Queen Elizabeth's coronation in 1953. A new social mythology emerged about Mount Everest. Scores of climbers from all over the world started to come annually for their own conquest of Mount Everest. About one in ten died in the attempt. The victims most often fell on the way down, which was the more hazardous part of the climb. Their frozen bodies lie preserved forever. No one knows the fate of climbers who attempted the climb from other directions in China and India. Climbing Mount Everest had become a daring fad for adventurous men from all over the world.

Thanks to her husband's involvement in royal politics, Tara had met Sir Hillary at one of numerous social gatherings. He was very accessible and many Nepalese could identify him walking about Kathmandu. Pasang would listen to Tara with fascination. All these things were another world to him. Life in Kathmandu could not be compared to his youth in a small farming settlement nearby

Lhasa. Life there was the same as it had been forever. How nice it would be to share these things in Nepal with Indus. Everything he saw and heard he related to Indus. Meanwhile, he had come to realize that Tara was well placed in social and political circles. He had more respect for her all the time, as well as affection. For Tara's part, she cared more for Pasang as he matured and became involved in the life of Nepal. She never forgot, however, that some time he would want to return home. Meanwhile, she would be as happy as she could.

Once a month at full moon they were affectionate all night and during the days in between there was genuine friendship between them. For Tara this was as much as she could expect from life within her Buddhist faith. For his part, Pasang kept thinking about Indus and Tibet. The Tibetans and their accounts stoked his desire to return in spite of the comfortable arrangement with Tara. He schemed about how he could earn money for his return and a better life back home with Indus. Tara sensed his anxieties, His hopes were encouraged by reports that border crossings were easier for those not wanted for agitation or criticism of China.

The Dalai Lama was comfortably established in India, surrounded by several thousand refugees. A little Tibetan society had emerged around him. The arrangement with the Indian government allowed him every freedom as long as his activities were not political. The Dalai Lama kept to the arrangement and indeed advised Tibetans to avoid controversies with China. His representatives kept up a dialogue with Chinese officials about how he might return to Tibet. He promised to act only as a religious leader and not a political head of state. Little came of these efforts to reach an agreement year after year. It seemed that China did not believe Tibetans would accept him only as a religious head of Buddhism, but rather as chief of state as well. China chose to bide its time.

International recognition of the Dalai Lama as a spokesman for peace, toleration, and spiritual values culminated in the Nobel

Prize for the Dalai Lama. China vehemently protested the award. This international recognition for the Dalai Lama strengthened China's resolve to keep the Nobel Prize winner out of Tibet. Meanwhile, China continued its efforts to absorb Tibet, even if it had been granted domestic self-government. The major world economic powers were so involved in lucrative trade with China that they made only token remarks in support of Tibet. Their sympathy for Tibet was restricted to welcoming Dalai Lama visits. He always spoke about spiritual enlightenment and peaceful relations between people wherever he traveled all over the globe. He respected the arrangement with India by avoiding remarks on politics, in hope of persuading Chinese officials to accept his return to Lhasa. In Nepal, close to India as it was, news about the Dalai Lama was common. The government in Nepal was studious in its efforts to maintain good relations with China, although it regularly complained to China about Maoist activities in Nepal.

The agitation for a communist society in Nepal was oddly enough out of date and somewhat pointless. Back in China a new economic policy had emerged. After some experimental free economic zones in southern China that offered free enterprise successfully, under strict regulation, the economy of China was gradually opening up to capitalism. Certain key components of the economy were kept under national ownership, but for the main part domestic and non-military economic activity was freed to operate on a profit basis along with taxation. What this meant for Tibet was that communes were gradually dissolved, and, like in the rest of China, a "responsibility" system for economic activity was allowed to flourish. Private land ownership was restored although some communes remained intact out of choice. Their new ventures were more efficient than single member ownership. This was a Chinese way of saying let free enterprise take hold. Reductions in religious harassment followed as well. News like this encouraged Pasang to prepare his return to Indus. He was glued to the TV when international news came on.

Tara welcomed Pasang's interest in earning money, although

she knew what he had in mind. Tara had a business of selling choice tea to a list of steady customers. Tea drinking was a major part of Nepalese life, as it was in Tibet. Tea was enjoyed several times a day. According to one's economic means, dozens of flavors were common and selected for different occasions and times of the day. People in Tibet cooked barley or oats blended with tea as a staple meal. Although it was not very nourishing, most people could afford this and little more.

Pasang became involved with tea growing and especially with managing harvests and marketing of Tara's production. Since tea terraces climbed up the mountain slopes ever higher, the production required much attention and handling of workers. Only the young leaves should be picked carefully so as to avoid hurting new growth. Pasang took easily to all these aspects of tea farming. He and Tara had become business partners. Every evening Pasang looked to the sky counting the days to full moon. In his mind he was feeling his love for Indus as he waited for Tara.

On one occasion he noted that Tara had workers mix some other dried leaves with a certain tea. This tea was packaged in a special colored wrapper for customers that paid a premium. Tara chuckled as she pointed out that some of this tea she would serve to Pasang when he would be getting ready for a nap. The special substance in the tea was cannabis, which helped produce relaxation and good feelings. Pasang immediately saw a business opportunity. Why not expand the sale of this special tea beyond Kathmandu? Tara's teas were marketed only in Kathmandu to this point. A new market would not hinder local sales, he felt.

It seemed like fate was in his favor when Torfu and his old smuggler mates came passing by Tara's property among the stream of travelers. Torfu had returned from India on a trading trip, and now he was looking for prospects in Kathmandu. The two met and enjoyed tea for a long while as they caught up with their lives. Pasang gave Torfu and his gang some of the special tea. They soon commented about its special qualities. Without telling Torfu more than he had to know, Pasang suggested that the two could start a business: Pasang would supply the choice tea that Torfu would sell beyond Kathmandu. This would avoid saturating the local market. Tara voiced no opposition as long as the tea bushes were not over-harvested. She wondered about Torfu's reliability, but after thinking it over, she and Pasang figured that Torfu's self-interest would keep him in check. After all, he would pay for the tea up front. How much he could sell it for in India was his affair. Once again Pasang thought of Indus and how he might return with a fistful of gold coins.

Torfu's group camped out on Tara's spacious property as the tea was harvested and blended under Pasang's careful attention. Care was taken to pack Pasang's blend in a distinctive wrapping to establish its identity. Pasang arranged to buy tea from other terrace owners to spare Tara's bushes, and he undertook to grow more of the cannabis on her land. Thus full moons came and went as Pasang tended to the means that would provide for his return to Indus.

Torfu had told him that there were Tibetans now serving among the border guards, and with bribes they were more lax than the Chinese at border inspections. All border guards took bribes, however. The guards had paid bribes to get an assignment as a border guard, so they had to make sure it was a good business. One matter was not subject to bribery, however. The guards had lists of wanted people, and they paid close attention to this as travelers went back and forth.

Tara introduced Pasang to another part of Nepalese life. At a social gathering the two met a group of New Zealanders who had just arrived to build primary schools. They had come with tools and power equipment to facilitate their work. After several months they would leave and their modern tools would stay behind. For the first time Pasang saw tall and pretty girls that were blond. It surprised him that the girls worked alongside the New Zealander boys like friends and equals. His knowledge of social relations was expanding. Tara just smiled as she saw him looking over the lovely

New Zealander girls.

Among the crowd celebrating a school opening Tara carefully pointed out some men among the crowd. "Those men are American government agents," she murmured. " I met them at a palace reception. They are here to do some things regarding Tibet, I'm not sure what. The king has given the American government permission to have some of its military people here. I can't imagine what good a few men can do here. Tibet is over the mountains and China is enormous."

Tara was well informed about political events thanks to her friends in government that dated back to when her husband was alive. Television news was current. However, she had little understanding of how Nepal and Tibet fit into global affairs. The Americans and North Vietnamese were in endless talks in Paris seeking a way to end the war in Vietnam. The American agents in Nepal were a small part of a vast international game of deadly chess.

The American president, Richard Nixon, was playing a surprising game. Secretary of State, Henry Kissinger, traveling through Pakistan, was on a secret visit to Beijing. A surprised Mao had agreed to host him and listen to what he had to say on behalf of the American president. Mao knew full well that President Nixon was a famous anti-communist. How could it be that he wanted to make friends with communist China? Everyone knew that his entire domestic political career had been based on virulent anti-communism. It turned out that now Nixon wanted to gain Chinese support to end the war in Vietnam. Moreover, he wanted to separate China from its close, but complicated, alliance with the Soviet Union. China had resented for many years that the Soviet Union refused to share nuclear technology with its communist ally. This grudge was not known to the United States, but it served to open the door to the unexpected conversations. Only such an audacious man as President Nixon could devise and attempt such a political move to alter global power relationships.

After greeting Chairman Mao, Kissinger put down a large and thick book on the table, saying, "Mr. Chairman, permit me to present The People's Republic to you." Before Mao could react to the audacious remark, Kissinger opened the book and revealed a large map of China. He explained that the multi-colored map was taken from outer space by American satellites. That map showed where in China there were deposits of iron. Mao peered down intently, noting some sites unknown to him. The same happened with other colored maps that located coal, copper, zinc, and other vital resources. "How come this shows water in the Gobi Desert?" Mao asked. Kissinger took pleasure displaying American intelligence about China. He noted that over millions of years snow melt poured north from Tibet and sank below the Gobi Desert sands. Agriculture could flourish in parts of the Gobi Desert. Mao was amazed, and then, looking deep into Kissinger's eyes for a long time, he stood up. He extended his hand. They shook hands warmly. China and the U.S. were now friends. Not long after, with China's support, an agreement was reached in Paris to end the war in Vietnam. To seal the bargain Nixon traveled to Beijin to meet with Chairman Mao the next year. Russian ties with China soon withered. Nixon's gift to Mao has never been made public, and foreign policy experts simply wondered at Nixon's genius in foreign affairs. How would the American public have reacted upon learning that their president had handed over some of the most secret American intelligence to the leader of China, against whom they had fought in Korea suffering many American casualties?

Not long after this shift in global power, Mao opened pilot areas for limited capitalism in southern China. The success of the pilot programs with limited capitalism led to the "responsibility" policy of free enterprise throughout China and Tibet. Mao figured that prosperity and trade with the United States would not endanger domestic political control. Europe and the world soon joined this new economic ballgame.

Pasang had a good business underway with the special teas he sold to Torfu. He shared the profits with Tara and these accumulated. Before long he was able to buy one small gold coin. More would follow as time went by. Tara did not need more money. She had what she needed and enjoyed high standing in Nepalese society. Her husband's memory was still held in high regard. She was careful when having Pasang accompany her to upper society affairs. He was presented as a business partner. Their intimate relationship was not public. He was not aware of these precautions, so it made no difference to him. He just worked hard at the tea business and kept track of the moon's phases. During the month he took warm baths prepared by the servants at his request. The older lady brought in a daughter to help scrub him over. After having his back done he would turn over and simply lay back in the warm water, close his eyes and think of Indus. The young girl was amazed at how his organ stood up as she washed it. The mother simply smiled as her daughter was introduced to pleasing a man. All the while Pasang thought of Indus. In time the mother chose other chores and let her daughter take care of Pasang when he wanted a bath. The daughter was agreeable.

Pasang was so dedicated to earning money selling his special tea that his dedication was obvious to Tara. She spoke to him in a soft manner calculated to ease his feelings. He had occasion to ask her why it was that nothing bothered or worried her. He knew that she had concerns, but she was always serene and accepting of whatever came about. He sometimes wondered how she would accept his eventual departure. Tara was an exceptional person.

Tara had observed that Pasang did not behave like a Buddhist, a Hindu, or like a member of any religion. She was acquainted with several religious practices common among people in Kathmandu and India. Pasang was different from Tibetans, all of whom were Buddhists. When she discretely asked him about what spiritual beliefs he had, he embarked into an account of his youthful friend Tao and the monastery where he was a novitiate. He told her about things he had forgotten over time. The gentle teachings of the old monk came back to mind. So too, the novitiates sitting down under a tree came back to mind. They spent the day reciting Buddhist prayers over and over again. He told Tara that all this had seemed silly to him, but that out of respect he had listened cordially to the old man.

Pasang somehow felt that he could rely more on Tara for wisdom than the old monk in the monastery. She was living in the real world, not in seclusion. Tara could sense that Pasang was wondering about spiritual matters, nonetheless. So she said that it was her belief that no one could orient him about such things, certainly not her. He had to think and feel in his own mind what life was about. Certainly Buddhist prayers and meditation would help him find his own way. She pointed out how that was essentially what the Buddha had done himself. On his own he concluded that his early life of comfort had little meaning and so he gave up all material things, including his own family. He began his life of wandering and contemplation. Tara told him that to her best understanding each person must find his own way. Pasang was thoughtful for a few minutes and then changed the subject.

Tara and Pasang went to a reception at the royal palace a few days later. Among the guests he heard people speaking languages he could not recognize, and dressed in various manners. Tara pointed out that King Birendra liked to mingle with people from all over the world. Kathmandu was a fashionable tourist site since the conquest of Mount Everest, and he enjoyed meeting interesting people who were important in their land. His staff took note of the tourists at the airport customs desk and helped make up a list of suitable guests. Because of the respect shown to Tara by important people, Pasang felt compelled to ask her why she got this treatment. While sipping some tea apart from the crowd she told Pasang that the respect shown to her was a remnant of her husband's position. As a noble and member of the royal council he was a major figure in Nepalese society. She was respected as his widow and because of her own personal background as well. Pasang gradually came to feel comfortable in upper society. Tara's acquaintances assumed he was a person of value simply because he was in her company. Pasang acted in the manner that he was treated. It was at this social affair that he realized he was becoming another person. How would he act and what would he do whenever he got back to Lhasa? He was mingling among Nepalese nobles and foreigners from all over the world. He was no longer the wretched young boy who fled over the Himalayas in fear for his life. Back at Tara's house he had two gold coins hidden away for his return to Indus, with more to follow.

Torfu was busy preparing the next shipment of the tea wrapped in yellow paper. His group would soon leave for India where he now had regular customers. After concluding their transaction, and before he left, the two friends talked about politics. Tara left them alone and simply made sure that her servants attended to them. She knew that Pasang lived for any news he could get about conditions in Tibet. Torfu had gone over the Dokar Pass into Tibet recently, thanks to more lenient controls at the border, but his profits now came mostly from selling Pasang's tea in nearby India. The friends parted and Pasang watched Torfu's group disappear over a ridge. He hoped that he too might be going over that same ridge on his way home. With this on his mind, he rubbed the newly acquired gold coin in his hand and thought of Indus. Maybe he could be traveling soon.

Tara was respectful of Pasang's new interest in religion. She went out of her way to show him where various religious groups gathered, and took him to the temples of some. Hindus, Muslims, Zoroastrians, as well as Buddhists had centers in Kathmandu. There were even some Jews and Christians. Tara knew her city well and what was going on there. Pasang had grown accustomed to cows and other stock roaming about the streets, unharmed due to religious taboos against hurting them. Luckily, some people not bound by their religion did slaughter animals and sold meat for eating. Tourists especially sought meat on the menu of hotel restaurants. On occasion Pasang would talk with people he noticed practicing a religion other than Buddhism. He was not a Buddhist, for that matter, he was simply curious about religion because of the way Tara was. He admired everything about her ways and understood all this came from her Buddhism. Waiting for a full moon to enjoy love was too long for him, however. He found pleasure asking for a warm bath and having the young girl wash him well and please him as he just closed his eyes and thought of Indus. In his fantasy the growing savings would give them a better life. He knew that the young girl was always willing and available. Giving Pasang pleasure gave her pleasure as well.

Watching television in the evening Tara and Pasang saw news that the Dalai Lama was nominated for the Nobel Prize and that China was vehemently protesting the award with vague and pointless threats. Some Tibetans in Kathmandu commented on television that this award would help the cause for independence from China. Others claimed it would only harden China's attitude to be shamed before the world by the honor bestowed on its opponent. Some international champions of Tibet, including some famous American movie actors, called for the United Nations finally to recognize Tibet as a nation and accept its longstanding application for membership. No major power had ever granted Tibet diplomatic recognition as a nation, and in the Security Council no motion was ever presented for Tibetan recognition since China promised a veto of any such motion. The Dalai Lama graciously accepted the award with good wishes for all peoples. The pair discussed whether this would affect Tibet and make it harder for Pasang's return. Tara spoke about his return casually for Pasang's benefit, but the idea was painful to her, so she privately hoped it would never come to pass. Pasang was an essential part of her life.

What precipitated Pasang's plans for a return was the totally unexpected appearance of Tao, his childhood friend who had joined the monastery of Jokhang. Once the world's largest monastery with several thousand monks, the Chinese government purged it like many others when the Dalai Lama fled to India. It was now a shell with only about 300 monks under watchful Chinese eyes. Because of its eminence Jokhang had been spared destruction, unlike hundreds of other monasteries. Tao fled Tibet like many others rather than find a way to earn a living for the first time. He had no occupation or skills. He could obtain work on construction jobs, but some included tearing down monasteries.

Tao had smuggled out his distinctive yellow robes. In Nepal Tibetans respected his robes and naturally gave him some of whatever food they had. Walking along the road on the way to downtown Kathmandu, Pasang saw the distinctive yellow robes of a Tibetan monk. Recognizing where the monk came from by the color of the robes, he quickly approached him to pay respects. Close at hand he recognized Tao. He took Tao home and gave him separate quarters, to Tara's delight. The pair talked late into the night as Pasang questioned Tao about affairs back home. Finally, Pasang could see that his guest was practically going to sleep sitting down after another long day's walk.

For days Tao and Pasang talked about conditions in Tibet. Television news frequently reported on Tibet. Tao had never seen television and was amazed. Pasang put on an act of sophistication. They heard reports about a remarkable meeting in India between the Dalai Lama and the Panchen Lama, two historical rivals for eminence in spiritual matters. The Panchen Lama had been cooperative with the Chinese, while the Dalai Lama had remained aloof, cordially insisting that he be allowed back to Tibet as a spiritual leader. The two mended fences and the Panchen Lama formally accepted the primacy of the Dalai Lama. The former rivalry dated back centuries, and the Chinese communists had increased friction between the two religious leaders by favoring the Panchen Lama. Spiritual leadership among Tibetans now seemed unified after this meeting. The meeting angered China, which suspected the worse intentions.

With funds from the Nobel Prize the Dalai Lama was free to travel the world, accepting one state visit after the other. Everywhere he made conciliatory remarks about China, hoping for the best. Finally, the Dalai Lama made a major formal statement, made known around the globe. He announced the renunciation of all and any secular authority in Tibet. In effect he retreated to being a simple monk, giving up the role of the Dalai Lama dating back a thousand years. He wanted to return to Tibet that much. While taking note of this declaration, China did not alter its position that the spiritual leader of Tibet is not welcome back to the Tibet Autonomous Region. China's stubbornness had paid off. Tibetans could no longer claim a chief of state.

While at a major temple in Kathmandu the two friends watched about 300 monkeys given free reign all over the temple. Nepalese accept the God Hamuman as guardian of the monkeys. This god is one of many animal gods in the eyes of Nepalese. Tao appears preoccupied to Pasang as they watch the interesting Nepalese customs. All these new Nepalese things were interesting to Tao, but his mind was elsewhere.

After much internal turmoil as to whether it is a good idea, Tao decides to bring up Indus. In a matter of fact way Tao asks Pasang if he recalls their mutual friend Indus. After all, many years have gone by since Tao helped Pasang escape Lhasa. Much to his pleasant surprise, Pasang pumps Tao for everything he knows about Indus. There was not much to tell. Tao heard from mutual friends that Indus had gone to live with Chang the noble. After the Chinese came Chang lost his land and serfs, but found a way to work with the new military government, Tao said. Tao learned that Chang died a few years later and Indus was left to live in his big house. That was all Tao had heard from friends that visited the monastery. Tao did not know about young Pasang. That was all Tao knew about Indus in spite of all the questions put by Pasang. Oh yes, he heard that she worked in a Chinese food restaurant called Green Lotus.

Pasang was on fire making plans for his return. He was no longer a poor Tibetan, and so to disguise himself he bought a ragged coat from a passing Tibetan. He proceeded to sew his gold coins into seams of the coat where they were well hidden from even a frisking. He would pay a bribe for crossing like everyone else, and even be reconciled to being robbed of whatever he had, as long as the five coins were safe. No guard would want his old coat, he figured.

Tao was also making plans for himself. He put aside his yellow robes that identified him as a member of a particular monastery. In Nepal he seemed disillusioned with the everyday discipline of a monk. Nepal was another world and he was willing to fit into it. He started dressing like an ordinary man. In his new life he had a place to live and all the necessary comforts in Tara's house. Tao worked on Tara's tea farm and enjoyed the work. Life in Nepal was affecting his religious beliefs. Tao thought about Shambala, the concept of an earthly paradise attributed to Buddha, but he never saw it in Nepal. However, Kathmandu and Nepal was the closest thing he had seen to Shambala. It did not occur to him that this might be a form of Shambala for him. The Nepalese government counted about 10,000 Tibetan refugees like him, and they may have felt the same about Nepal. Here the soil was so fertile that two crops per year were common. Some Tibetans were renting land to farm and working in various occupations, despite resentment from Nepalese because they worked for less.

Over time Tibetan monks had built several monasteries and one nunnery from donations. In some respects Tao found himself living in a part of Tibet abroad, just over the Himalayas. Nonetheless, a different life was starting to make him different. Pasang noticed the changes in his childhood friend but said nothing.

Pasang persuaded Tao to help him with the tea business that was prospering. Tao had never done manual labor as a monk but he took to it happily. He confessed to Pasang that he might never go back to Tibet because the life of a Buddhist monk was progressively being undone by social change, as well as by Chinese harassment. Before the Chinese came there were about 6,000 monasteries with several hundred thousand monks. In Tibet monks now numbered about 1,000 in a few monasteries, Tao estimated. The giant Potala Palace and Jokhang monasteries in Lhasa were not typical of the fate suffered by others. Indeed both had been rejuvenated and looked like new. Chinese and other tourists flocked to see them. For centuries the Potala palace had been strictly reserved for monks attending the Dalai Lama. Now tourists could enjoy tea and snacks at a restaurant at the very top of the Potala monastery. From that rooftop they could see the majestic mountains around the valley of Lhasa.

For Tibetans the Potala Palace was the residence of the Goddess of Mercy. Built by a Tibetan king for his beloved wife centuries ago, it was expanded over time and came to hold not only the residence of the Dalai Lama, but in the second part, about 1,000 halls used for meditation and storage of ancient records. Under the new Tibetan regime there were far more tourists visiting the palace in one day than monks still living there. Although UNESCO had declared the Potala Palace a "World Heritage Site," Tao felt that the Tibet he grew up in was no longer there for him to see again.

Tao was also feeling less calling for the social functions of a monk. Perhaps the many new things in Nepal were distracting him from the state of mind that his studies and meditation had been instilling in him. Perhaps it was the food, customs, free social relations, news about the world, and of course living in the house of Tara. In Tibet believers regularly approached a monk like him for personal help, such as predicting their future or advice on a business matter. After some recitations and prayers, a monk might well pronounce his advice, "Do not dispose of something with value," with no fear of a mistake. This sort of function now seemed to have less attraction to Tao. Thus he no longer wore the beautiful yellow robes, to avoid identification. It was odd that one of two old friends was feeling attraction to spiritual matters while the other was feeling them slip away.

A few days after a full moon and their love, Pasang found the courage to tell Tara that he had decided to return to Lhasa despite the risks. She was not surprised, although saddened. She had noticed a change in Pasang ever since Torfu had told them that border controls were more relaxed now that separatist actions in

Tibet had lessened. Their normal routine was brought to an end when Torfu returned from India a week later. He was ready to buy another shipment of Pasang's tea. When Pasang told him about his plans Torfu offered to assign two men to accompany him up the mountains to a favorable crossing post. His men would know what to do in order to handle the delicate crossing situation. In response to Pasang, Torfu explained that one of the men would cross first while the other and Pasang waited for signals as to what hour of the day Tibetans managed the border crossing. Chinese were less predictable to deal with and demanded larger bribes. A small hand mirror would flash the signal and the two men would then approach the crossing. Torfu assured Pasang that the crossing back into Tibet should be routine.

Pasang felt his long, old jacket for the five gold coins he sewed into the seams in a way that they could not be felt. Tara had helped him finish the sewing as he prepared other things. Among these was giving all his personal effects to Tao since he would stay in Tara's house. Pasang would look like a poor Tibetan when the guards examined him. Tara cleverly suggested that one new and obvious patch be made on the jacket under an armpit. Within it she placed some Nepalese coins and one small gold, as if hidden. If the guards were thorough and noticed this patch, they might tear it off and find the hidden treasure. Pasang went along with Tara's scheme. She always knew what to do.

The night before the crossing the moon was not full yet, but Pasang and Tara decided to enjoy each other just the same. All along the tortuous climb wending back and forth out of the lovely valley, Pasang thought of Tara and all her kindness to him over the years the two were together. The first night on the trail out of Nepal he recalled that she was living proof about the power of love, as her Buddhist beliefs said. True love was far beyond personal gratification like his, when Tara first saw him alongside her wall. She never tried to persuade him about anything, she simply lived a life of moderation and love for him. He wondered whether there was anything to beliefs about destiny. He had thoughts about such things as the three men climbed up the slopes, the majestic Himalayas always higher up. He recalled seeing Tara and Tao far below standing close together. They were holding hands and waving as Pasang walked on. They slipped out of sight. He had happy thoughts for the two. As the trail turned and faced north looking at the pass into Tibet, all at once his only thoughts were of Indus and that she worked at a restaurant called The Green Lotus.

Early the next morning his guide pointed to a flashing mirror far ahead. It was time to go. There were numerous border crossers in line and this helped them. The guards would be anxious to get rid of the crowd. After looking up the names of the two and not finding them among the wanted, the guards passed the pair on to personal inspection. . Pasang chuckled to himself that crossers could use any name, and that the Tibetan guards must know this. The guards searched for hand weapons, anxious to keep these out of Tibet. After paying the fees and offering a generous tip, the pair thought the crossing was done. A second guard in a bad mood appeared and patted down the pair, feeling for arms a second time. He was more thorough and saw the patch that looked newer than the rest of the old jacket. Sure enough, upon tearing the patch open he found the Tibetan coins and the gold one as well. He silently slipped into these in to his pocket, with a smiling look at Pasang. The happy guard waved the pair on and they set off into Tibet. The trail now sloped downward and Pasang wore a big smile as they trudged along. His companion could not fully appreciate the smile. With his assignment done for Torfu, with Pasang safely back in Tibet, the guide bid farewell and turned back towards Nepal.

CHAPTER SEVEN
HOME IN LHASA

Young Pasang and Chu saw each other frequently, and in the company of the professor the trio became a fixture at The Green Lotus. The professor liked to talk about many things and the young couple just listened to the fountain of knowledge and political information. The professor commented at length about the friction over the plans underway to establish a university in Lhasa. The Socialist Educational Movement in Beijing continued to recruit hundreds of Tibetan youths to study in China. The professor hoped that in Tibet the new university would concentrate on research, leaving the practical arts and education for centers in China. By studying in China Tibetans would become more attached to the Motherland. The two youths had been part of the program for studies in China. They did not comment to the others whether they had become more sympathetic to China by studying in Chengdu, but they both now had a practical vocation of much value in Tibet. They were grateful for China's educational help while not thinking about the global aspects of Chinese policy.

The professor felt relaxed with the young people and, perhaps because they were not in China proper, he commented sarcastically about politics in Beijing. The professor was from Sichuan, and people from Sichuan Province were noted for independence. They looked down on politicians in the capital. The professor was critical of Chinese efforts to build nuclear capability beyond simple production of electric energy. Through the grapevine of professors, he learned that China was incensed with the Soviet Union because it had refused repeatedly to share nuclear research information with the Motherland. China was forced to advance its nuclear capability on its own and with espionage it practiced abroad.   The professor observed that Soviet distrust of China was now mutual although both giants were communists. This uneasy alliance probably explained China's budding friendship with the United States. In any case, he noted, the new foreign policy would be very beneficial. Along with new trade and exchanges in the field of education, perhaps American investments could help speed up economic development in China. The professor noted that through education the Motherland could in time peacefully shed the iron grip of one party rule. He looked at the young pair and solemnly told them that they were the future for a better Motherland than what Marxism offered. Pasang Junior regarded the professor with a puzzled look at that remark. The professor took note of that and said firmly, he did not believe in any ideology, he believed only in himself. He continued, China has had two giants in its long history, Confucius and Mao Zedong. Confucius would outlast Mao, he whispered with conviction. Lovely Chu smirked between sips of Chinese soup, and surprisingly, she said nothing. Revealing the success of Chinese indoctrination, she wondered aloud what country would be crazy enough to threaten China.

The professor went on to say that not all threats were foreign. Islamic Chinese posed a dilemma in the western regions because some had connections with Iran. They got financial support and encouragement from Teheran to extend their influence and culture. Since their speech in temples was in Farsi, Chinese authorities were ignorant of what their Imams said. The government knew that elsewhere in Islamic regions Imans were active political commentators and sometimes incited their congregations to take violent actions against individual disbelievers. This was no attack on the Motherland, the professor noted, but Islam posed a distinct menace just the same. These discussions went on for hours now and then. The servants just kept bringing more tea.

Indus was becoming accustomed to seeing the young pair as she walked about the restaurant attending to customers. She was happy to learn that Chu's parents operated a beauty salon. In keeping with common practice, it had a section for Han women and one for Tibetans. Some Tibetan women with means were now caring for their appearance like the Han women. They took facials, hair grooming, and used makeup like the Hans. Chinese and western clothing were becoming common among Tibetans in Lhasa, rather than the traditional garments commonly found in the countryside. Remembering the way she and Pasang looked at each other a long time ago, Indus saw the young couple looking at each other in the same way. It made her happy to remember the same thing.

General Li came back after two weeks in Beijing. He was particularly attentive to Indus and stayed in bed with her more than usual. She was happy with this, but figured that something was on his mind because he was so attentive. Li came home every night and their relations had the appearance of a honeymoon. They were alone because Pasang Junior was off into the vast Qinghai plateau looking into herding conditions. This vast region was rarely monitored by the Tibetan authorities before, or even by the Chinese now. Much was needed to make the remote region more productive and Pasang's work was part of this effort.

In the morning after one happy night of love, Li finally bursts out with the news that he has been called back to Beijing. When Indus asked for how long, as she always did, he paused a long time. He then said very deliberately, "Indus, I have a new assignment and I will not be coming back." As she tried to absorb the impact of his words, he said that the transfer was to a vital post in Mongolia, near Islamic unrest. " Can you imagine, I will be going home." He could not refuse the appointment, and must leave in three days. He would barely have time to prepare his staff to take over until his replacement arrived.

Indus looked at Li with an obvious question in her eyes. Answering the unspoken question, he said that he must go alone, that she cannot follow him because of regulations. Although Indus looked shocked at the news, Li had no way of knowing that Indus would never have gone with him, even if it were possible. Granted, his rank and social position would have created a life difficult for her to cope with. But what mattered most of all, she would have to give up her life in Lhasa and the hope that Pasang would come back to her. Indus must be where Pasang could find her.

In any case, Li would not have taken her and Pasang with him, not as a mistress and certainly not as a wife. The fact that she was Tibetan was decisive. His professional future called for a marriage to the daughter of a well-placed Chinese Han family. Such a wife could give him what he wanted more than anything, a son. If Indus had not been sterile, maybe things might have been different, but not likely. She was Tibetan.

Li tells Indus that a short farewell is best because he is truly sorry to leave. She was the only woman to have shared his every thought and feeling for some ten years. Indus was a part of him. He hugs her strongly and quickly walks out of the house before the stunned Indus can do anything but watch him go. After a short distance, Li stops and turns around to see Indus. She is standing at the door. He looks at her a long time, then turns again and practically runs away.

CHAPTER EIGHT
RETURN TO INDUS

As his two guides headed back towards Kathmandu, their job done, Pasang proceeded northward towards Lhasa. There were tough climbs now and then, but on the way home, with the mighty Himalayas at his back, he never tired and felt like singing. The land was now barren and he longed for the green fields of Nepal. Being in familiar land made up for that. Camping overnight in the open was uncomfortable since his supplies were next to nothing. The border guards took what little he had. On the second day he came to a monastery that was partially destroyed, and yet it was surrounded by hundreds of people in a festive mood. It was New Years. He had lost track of the Tibetan religious calendar while in Nepal for so long. The Great Summons Ceremony would last for a couple of weeks, and in Lhasa even longer, with many thousands of worshipers coming from great distances. Two long and elaborate horns about four meters long blasted sounds he was familiar with. Their deep sounds were beautiful and audible for great distances. Their echoes came back to hear again. What he had not encountered before, however, was the tapestry laid out on a hillside. It stretched out more than an American basketball court. It was one piece and woven with colorful figures and writing he could not understand. The sound of the horns and the beautiful tapestry made him feel very proud to be Tibetan. It astounded him to learn that the enormous tapestry was centuries old. Somehow it had survived both time and Chinese vandalism directed at diminishing such elements of Tibetan religious culture.

The monastery must have been large and important to merit such art works, but there was only a small number of monks living there now. He approached an old monk to inquire about the site. The old monk told him how the Chinese ordered its demolition, using some soldiers and the monks themselves, not long after the Dalai Lama fled to India. Pasang asked how the horns and tapestry survived. The old monk said that many valuable records and volumes of written prayers also survived due to the grace of the gods that had protected the ancient monastery. The tapestry was the most valuable treasure saved. Everything else was burned, if not broken up. The old monk told how, thanks to the gods, the Chinese commander turned out to be Buddhist as were some of the soldiers. He ordered the soldiers to look the other way as the monks buried the treasure under trash from the demolition. The monks were all driven away to earn their living as best they could. Now, a few had come back. Fortunately, thanks to new policy, the old man told Pasang, the monastery was on a list for restoration. The monks could therefore bring out the horns and tapestry. As Tibetans learned about the pending restoration, they gathered around the monastery for festivals like never before.

The festival dancing went on for hours to drive away the devils. Pasang enjoyed the horse racing. He knew that the races had a religious function as much as they thrilled the crowds. Much commercial activity was taking place among the worshipers as well. These crowds grew in numbers as the horns blasted far away, attracting more.

Among the dancers spinning around in a circle one young girl stopped for a moment to look straight into Pasang's eyes. He was shocked at her resemblance to Indus. She smiled at him with a "would you like to," look. Then she danced on with the group. Before she could come around again, he turned, and pushing his way through the crowd, he left the ceremonies walking firmly towards Lhasa. The pretty and bold girl only made him want to push on.

Pasang camped out alongside the enormous river that came down from the Himalayas, passing by Lhasa. He was in familiar land as he approached the outskirts of Lhasa. Looking around thoroughly in the morning to be sure he was alone, he cut open the coat to bring out the coins he and Tara had woven in carefully. He counted his five gold coins out loud as if to make sure they were all there. But to his surprise there were three more gold coins, larger than the ones he had gathered. He thought for only a moment, and then he recalled that Tara had insisted on finishing the sewing on the old coat. His heart swelled with love for Tara, and his eyes got wet as he recalled the years with her. For some reason he also remembered seeing Tara and Tao standing close side by side as they smiled and waved goodbye to him.

He resumed his walk into the city. The tall buildings were new to him, and they reminded him of Kathmandu. The streets of Lhasa were well paved, and before long he was walking on a wide sidewalk with many cars running by, as well as carts and trucks loaded with all sorts of goods, like in Kathmandu. This was a new Lhasa in many ways, chiefly in that half the people walking around were Chinese. His resentment was overcome by the knowledge that he would soon be with Indus, if only he could find The Green Lotus restaurant.

A pretty Tibetan girl came up to him and boldly asked if he wanted her company. She quickly made it clear what she had in mind. Pasang had never heard of prostitution in Lhasa, so the encounter and the girl interested him. She readily accepted his invitation for a cup of tea. The girl gobbled up the sweet bread he ordered and readily accepted a second portion. She obviously was very hungry. With her stomach full and warm she talked pleasantly in order to entice the potential client. She was a talkative girl with a pleasant voice. She and the situation fascinated him. She talked on, assuming that he was listening.

Pasang's mind wanders back to Nepal as the girl talks on. Torfu had returned from a successful trip to India selling Pasang's tea. With his earnings he invited Pasang to a nice whorehouse in the city where they knew him as a regular customer. Ugly as he was, the ladies liked him because he tipped generously. Pasang firmly refused the prospect of bedding with a woman, out of loyalty to Tara. Torfu persuaded him to go along if only to see for himself. The house was nicely furnished with numerous good-looking women and girls sitting around, talking with potential clients. From time to time a pair would go off to a bedroom. Bedding a lady was not necessary for clients. They often simply enjoyed a while of pleasant company. The ladies were well dressed and very well informed about current affairs, providing conversation to suit the clients. Pasang thought this was rather sophisticated as he waited for Torfu to finish with his lady of choice this time around.

Torfu enjoyed telling Pasang about how he finally persuaded Tao, now that he was a former monk, to accompany him to the house. When Tao bashfully admitted that he had never been with a woman, Torfu assured him that he would be his guest and need only converse with some charming girl. The conversation in the living room with tea and sweet bread was interesting to Tao, and he did enjoy the company, but he held off picking a girl to bed with. Torfu alerted one of his favorite ladies to Tao's virginity. The experienced lady rubbed her hands, and with a smile, she boldly took Tao by the hand and led him off to a room before he knew how to decline. He was back in a while wearing a big smile. Torfu laughed, holding his stomach in pleasure as he told the story about the former monk.

At that point of the reverie, the pretty girl put the question to Pasang. Would he go with her, or not? She pointed out that, if not, her handler would charge her his part of her fee since he had seen them enter the teahouse and just waste time. Her handler was a Han and controlled this side of the avenue. Her working space was the sidewalk from one intersection to another. Pasang chuckled at the situation, and understandably paid her fee and added a healthy tip. They parted company and Pasang resumed his search for The Green Lotus.

A helpful Tibetan told Pasang that The Green Lotus was in fact just across the avenue (the sign was in Mandarin which Pasang could not read). Amazed at his luck he approached the restaurant and entered cautiously. The clients were all Han and well dressed, but so was he in the clothing he had just bought. Once inside he waited for the maître d' to seat him. Thanks to Kathmandu and Tara, he knew the routine at good eating places.

Indus saw him first. She came over to him in disbelief. The years had not changed his appearance much. Tibetans do not hug each other, but Nepalese do. Pasang jumped up, called her name loudly, and then hugged her firmly for a long time, without another word. All the clients saw them, and wondered who this man was. The Tibetan waiters also wondered what this was all about. After all, Indus was their proprietor, and they associated her with Lt. General Li. Who was this stranger hugging Indus? Both Indus and Pasang were in a trance after fifteen years of separation. They were oblivious to everything around them. They just kept hugging.

Indus at last said, "Come with me, there is something I want you to see". She led him just out of town to where she lived. Her pigpens were nearby. She explained why the pens were so extensive. "Hans love pork, you know". She also explained, to his amazement, that she was not an employee, but owned The Green Lotus. He did not know what to say. At this point he stopped and pulled out the eight gold coins and showed them to her. He wanted her to see that he too was a man of means. She gasped at their value and fondled the three larger gold coins. She wondered how to invest them then and there.

They approached the pigpens where a young man had just laid a layer of new straw in one pen, and covered it with a wool blanket. Indus asked Pasang to ask the young man to come to her. When Pasang approached, the boy turned around. Pasang saw himself standing there at the age he fled Tibet. The two men just looked at each other for a long time. Pasang then turned to Indus and asked timidly, " Is he mine?" Indus took her time, and then said emphatically, "Nooo…, he is ours!" The men hugged each other tightly in silence, and then Indus hugged both. The three stood there a long time.

They walked towards the house holding hands without saying a word. Unexpectantly, Chu walked up to greet them. She said joyfully that her long tour giving vaccinations in the countryside was over and she was now free for a week. Chu then looked at the stranger, wondering who he was since he was hugging Indus. Noting Chu's curiosity, Indus proudly told her that he was Pasang's father. Chu was speechless, which was not common for her. She looked back and forth at the two and saw the resemblance. She then huddled up close to her own Pasang, looking at his father with wonder.

Hand in hand the four walked back towards the house. The evening sky was clear and the bright moon was almost full. After some conversation young Pasang asked for permission to leave because he and Chu had some things to do. Chu had been away for many days and the two wanted to be together. Indus and Pasang wanted to be alone anyway, so they agreed. The young couple headed towards the pigpens. Indus said with a smile, " I don't think they will spend much time counting stars tonight. They love each other very much."

Indus led Pasang into the large house, which was now hers. Upon entering, Pasang took note of the big stairway leading up to the bedrooms. Somehow the stairway reminded him of the American movie he had seen on TV with Tara in Kathmandu. In the movie about the American civil war the hero scoops up the heroine and storms up the stairs to the bedroom where they make passionate love. Indus gasps as Pasang scoops her up and strides up the stairs like in the movie. At the upper landing Indus points in the right direction and Pasang carries her through the bedroom door. He will not wait for a full moon ever again.

The End

JULIAN NAVA

Professor Julian Nava has traveled in China from Jilin in the far north to Tibet in the south, as well to lands around the globe. A retired Professor of History and author of numerous books for schools and college, he also published his autobiography, My Mexican American Journey.

Nava concluded that a historical novel was the best way to tell about the changes taking place in the Himalayas since the People's Republic of China took control of Tibet in 1950. Some elements of the novel contain information Nava learned from the CIA while serving as a U.S. ambassador. The world has followed the drama of the Dalai Lama and his efforts to preserve Tibet's ancient autonomy.

As winner of the Nobel Peace Price, the Dalai Lama enjoys the respect and sympathy of people around the globe. The events in Tibet are complicated and involve valid conflicting evaluations of China's role, which the novel portrays. The author hopes that the novel helps promote greater understanding and good will, while telling a moving love story that embodies the events that have taken place in Tibet.

After service in World War II, Nava entered college under the GI Bill. After a degree from Los Angeles Community College, then Pomona College and Harvard, where he gained a Ph.D., he went on to teach in Puerto Rico, Spain, Colombia, and California State University Northridge, from which he retired in 2000. A political activist, Nava has deep affection for peoples like the Tibetans. He identifies with some of their experiences. He continues active in social and political affairs after serving as U.S. Ambassador to Mexico, appointed by President Jimmy Carter.

Nava lives on a small horse ranch in Valley Center, California, with his wife of fifty-two years Patricia. Nearby his three children are all educational professionals as well.

WPR BOOKS has been publishing books and directories since 1983. WPR Books has seven imprints: *Comida, Helping Hands, Heroes, Latino Insights, Latin American Insights, Para los Niños,* and *Total Success.* **WPR BOOKS** is dedicated to improving portrayals and expanding opportunities for Latinos in the USA.

For more on these & other books, go to www.WPRbooks.com

Another great book by Julian Nava from **WPR** Books

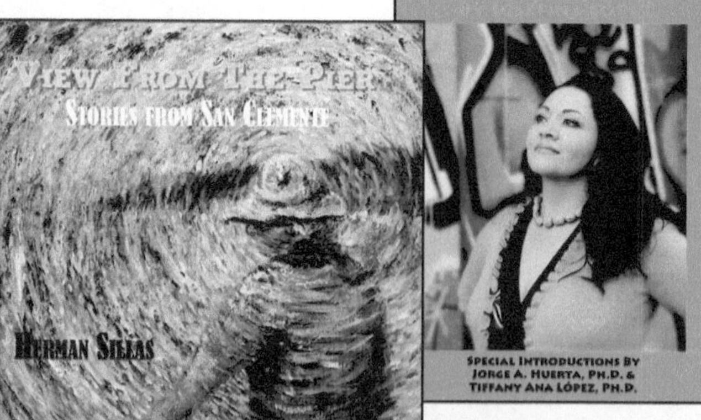